# BET ON Love

## DEVON VAUGHN ARCHER

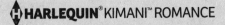

**HARLEQUIN**® KIMANI™ ROMANCE

To "Beautiful Mermaid," the love of my life who was a sure bet as someone I wanted as my bride and best friend. Thank you for being there for what seems like forever. Our best years are still ahead of us.

And to my mother, Marjah A. Flowers, sister, Jacquelyn V. White, nieces, and other ladies who believe in the power of love and romance in the world of fiction and real life.

Recycling programs
for this product may
not exist in your area.

ISBN-13: 978-0-373-86340-2

BET ON LOVE

Copyright © 2014 by R. Barri Flowers

For questions and comments about the quality of this book please contact us at CustomerService@Harlequin.com.

**Printed in U.S.A.**

Dear Reader,

I am delighted to present to you my latest Harlequin Kimani Romance novel, *Bet on Love,* as part of the Kimani Hotties: Promise Me Forever series.

Reporter Bianca Wagner is not much of a gambler, but when she makes a connection with handsome Las Vegas Strip casino owner Tanner Long, all bets are off! Rolling the dice becomes even more challenging when Bianca becomes pregnant and wants the winning hand before she gives in to all-consuming love.

The idea for this story came from a desire to build a romance amid the glamour, glitz and gambling in one of the world's most dynamic cities.

Here's a secret about the heroine, Bianca: she is the sister of Madison Wagner, the heroine of my previous Harlequin Kimani romance, *Say It with Roses,* in which Bianca made an appearance.

You are sure to find this charming love story an enjoyable read from start to finish!

I also invite you to read my recent Hawaii-themed Harlequin Kimani romances, *Aloha Fantasy, Private Luau* and *Pleasure in Hawaii.*

Kind regards,

Devon Vaughn Archer

I would like to thank my wife, H. Loraine, for her diligent devotion to me and my writings. I daresay I would never be where I am today as a successful author without your encouragement and support.

I also extend appreciation to all the Harlequin editors and staff that I have worked with over the years for their professionalism and friendship.

# Chapter 1

Bianca Wagner felt exhausted, yet invigorated, when she got back to her two-story Spanish-style Las Vegas home on Tenaya Way after an early morning jog. She had just enough time to jump in the shower, grab a quick breakfast and head to work. It was a routine Bianca had perfected, along with spending long hours at home—often alone—and less time hanging out with friends. Admittedly, she would welcome the right male companion into the equation, but since that had been hard to come by of late, she chose to focus her attention elsewhere. Such as on maintaining her health at age thirty-three, both physically and mentally.

Bianca got dressed, put on her makeup and brushed her long blond hair with brown highlights. She grabbed a bagel and her travel coffee cup as she headed out the door and into her Subaru Legacy. She was an arts-and-entertainment reporter with the *Vegas Valley Happen-*

*ings* newspaper. She'd taken the assignment six months ago after previously being the crime-and-courts reporter. Though she missed covering criminality in Sin City, she loved reporting on the city's rich arts-and-entertainment scene.

Suddenly Bianca's cell phone rang, interrupting her thoughts. She took a quick glance and saw that it was her sister, Madison. Smiling, Bianca turned on the speakerphone.

"Hey, sis."

"Hey," Madison said cheerfully. "We just got back from a bike ride and I thought I'd give you a quick call."

Bianca considered the "we" in her sister's statement. That would be Madison and her husband of one year, Stuart. He had two lovely little twin daughters from a previous relationship, who often accompanied them on their bike rides.

*Why can't I be so lucky to have a gorgeous guy who adores me with all his heart?* Bianca asked herself.

"I appreciate the call," she told Madison. "But I'm on my way to work and the traffic is… Well, you saw how it is when you and Stuart were here last year on your honeymoon."

"Oh, yes, I remember," Madison said. "Call me later?"

"I will. And give the girls a big kiss for me."

"Count on it," Madison promised.

Bianca disconnected. She focused on the road, but couldn't help but think that her younger sister seemed to have it all these days, which left Bianca to play catch-up.

*Will I ever have everything Madison does?* She could only hope. On the other hand, as a career-minded woman, would she ever truly be ready to take on the responsibilities of raising a family? Unlike Madison, maybe she simply wasn't cut out to be a mommy.

Turning onto South Las Vegas Boulevard toward downtown, Bianca thought about the latest big news to hit the city—the upcoming opening of the Aloha Seas Hotel and Casino on the Strip. From what she'd heard, it would be like visiting the tropical paradise of Maui, with gambling and other Vegas-style entertainments as added attractions. Having been to Hawaii a couple of times, she was looking forward to the resort's opening, both as a reporter and someone who couldn't get enough of the islands.

The Aloha Seas' principal owners were brothers, Tanner and Solomon Long. They were both handsome and seemed to alternate years being voted the most eligible bachelor in Las Vegas. From what Bianca had seen, they had beautiful women on their arms every other day as they enjoyed the perks of wealth, good looks and undeniable charm.

*If that's how they prefer to get their kicks, that's their problem,* she thought, while doubting either one saw it as a problem.

She had more worries than spending too much time thinking about spoiled, rich casino owners. For example, was she ever going to escape this traffic jam and get to work?

Tanner Long sat in the backseat of his limousine, talking on the phone to his brother, Solomon. As usual, they were at odds on how to do things, while trying to keep the peace as they took on their latest venture. This venture happened to be a very big one. There were only two days until the grand opening of Aloha Seas, the newest hotel and casino on the Las Vegas Strip. As the majority owners, they had pooled their resources and gotten the right investors to roll the dice, so to speak, on making this new casino a big success.

But seeing eye to eye on the details took patience on Tanner's part and seemingly more give than take, as he wanted this event to go without a hitch.

"You only have one grand opening, little brother," Tanner argued in his role as chief executive officer. "And that means we need to make a splash while the attention is squarely on us."

"I hear you," Solomon said sharply. "And I agree. But that doesn't mean we need to break the bank in the process. Cutting corners can be done without cutting the quality of the grand opening."

Tanner chuckled. It seemed as if they were just going around in circles. At thirty-six, he was a year older and maybe a few years wiser than his brother. Or so he tried to convince himself. But, then again, Solomon did have an MBA and was the chief operating officer. Tanner's degree was in hotel management with a minor in marketing. Rather than continue to bump heads, he gave in.

"All right, do whatever you think needs to be done— just don't screw this up."

"I won't," Solomon assured him. "I want this to work as much as you do, if not more."

"I know," Tanner conceded. Both had spent much of their lives trying to follow in the footsteps of their father, a very successful businessman. He and their mother would have been really proud to see just how much they had accomplished up to this point. *I'm just glad they lived to see us receive our degrees and start building our legacy,* Tanner thought.

Before he could cut the call short, the limousine suddenly shook violently and Tanner heard a loud thump as they came to a halt.

"What the hell…" The words spewed from his mouth.

He heard something similar from his driver, Johan.

"What's going on?" Solomon asked.

"Looks like we've been in an accident," Tanner said irritably.

"Are you all right?"

"I'm fine," Tanner said. "Don't know if I can say the same about the limo, though. I'll call you back."

Tanner hung up. "What happened?" he asked Johan.

"The car ahead of me stopped suddenly. I slammed on the brakes, but couldn't slow down enough."

"Great! Just what I need," Tanner grumbled. He watched Johan open the driver's door and get out, then followed. Tanner stepped onto South Las Vegas Boulevard, jam-packed with vehicles that were now at a standstill, and made his way to the front of the limo. A cursory glance told him that the damage was relatively minor.

When he looked at the other vehicle, a red Subaru Legacy, it was clear that it had sustained the worst damage from the collision.

He watched as the Subaru's driver got out and approached him. "I'll handle this," he told Johan before turning his attention to the female driver. She was tall by female standards, though still about eight inches shorter than his six-foot-four frame. Her blond, brown streaked hair was long and wavy, and she had nice lips that were presently a crooked line, but that didn't stop him from finding her drop-dead gorgeous.

She gazed at her vehicle and then glared at him. "Look what you did to my car!"

"Actually, it was my driver," Tanner said humorlessly, glancing at Johan. "Technically speaking. Beyond that, you didn't exactly give him a choice with your sudden stop."

"I stopped because a car swerved into my lane," she snapped. "It would have hit me if hadn't slammed on the brakes. Maybe if your driver hadn't been riding my bumper for a couple of blocks, he would have had more time to react."

Johan furrowed his brow. "You're blaming me for this?"

She turned her brown eyes to him. "The damage speaks for itself."

Tanner got between them as if they were ready to come to blows. He looked ahead of her car and saw that traffic had begun to move again, including the careless driver who had apparently been responsible for this entire mess. He didn't doubt that she was telling the truth, knowing how crazy some of the drivers were in Vegas, but that didn't change their situation.

"Well, what's done is done," Tanner told the attractive woman.

"What about the damage to my car?" she asked tartly.

"Isn't that what your insurance is for?" Tanner asked.

"Yes, when it's my fault. Other than that, I'd rather not have to go through my insurance company, only to have my rates go up unfairly."

"I see." Tanner put a hand to his chin. Though there was no way of knowing who truly was at fault for the damage outside of the other driver, he decided to cut her some slack. But only because he was in a hurry and didn't want to drag this thing out any longer than necessary. Besides, a buddy of his owned an auto repair shop and owed him a favor. Now, with two cars that needed work, he would owe his friend a favor. "We'll take care of it, no problem. I can call for a tow to take your car to be repaired and give you a lift anywhere you like."

"Fine," she said with seeming reluctance, as though he planned to kidnap her in broad daylight.

"By the way, I'm Tanner Long and this is my driver, Johan."

"Bianca Wagner."

Tanner took out his cell phone and met her eyes. *This ought to be interesting,* he thought. Maybe in more ways than one.

Bianca sat in the limousine, wondering if she would have been better off simply driving her car to the repair shop herself. But why should she? The rear end of her car was damaged, through no fault of her own, and Tanner Long was footing the bill to have it repaired.

She glanced at him as he sat next to her, checking her out. Pretending not to notice, she turned away. But the image of him was indelibly seared in her mind. After all, she'd seen him enough on television, the paper and online. In person, he was even more gorgeous, if that was even possible. Tall and trim, he was bald with chiseled features, gray-black eyes, a thin mustache and small chin beard. His business-casual attire was a perfect fit and suited him.

*I'd love to ask him a few questions about himself and his business success,* she thought, *but I wouldn't want him to get any more conceited than he probably already is.* Especially since she was vulnerable as his passenger and a car-accident victim, rather than being here in her professional capacity.

"Where are you from?" Tanner asked, as if strictly for conversation.

"Excuse me?" Bianca's eyes widened.

"It doesn't sound like you're from around here."

"What does my voice sound like to you?" She was curious, considering she believed she had no accent.

"It sounds sexy," Tanner said, a half grin playing on his lips. "Aside from that, I think I detected a slight Southern inflection there. Maybe from Texas, Georgia, or Alabama. Am I getting close?"

*Too close,* Bianca thought. "Actually, I'm from Houston," she confessed.

He smiled. "Houston's a great city. How long have you been in Vegas?"

"Awhile," she responded, deciding to turn the tables. "Where are you from?" She seemed to recall that she'd read he was from the East.

"New York," he said. "I loved it there, but my brother and I needed to chart our own territory, so we ended up here in Vegas."

"Good for you." Bianca paused thoughtfully. "And your brother is Solomon Long…?"

"Yeah, you know him?"

"Only of him—and you," she said tonelessly. "I read the papers."

"I see." Tanner sat back. "So are you a gambler?"

Bianca met his eyes. "Not really. I only like to bet on a sure thing."

He laughed. "Yeah. Me, too."

She colored under the weight of his stare, as though she were that "sure thing" in his mind. Or was she misreading him as a man who was used to getting who and what he wanted?

"Is that why you're opening up a casino?" she asked.

"Good question," Tanner said. "Actually, I do consider it a sure thing. People come from all over the world to Las Vegas to gamble, among other things. There's always room for one more place to spend and lose money."

"Aloha Seas," Bianca said.

"You've got it." He smiled. "If you'd like to come to the grand opening in two days, consider this an invitation."

"Thanks, but I'll be busy that day," she responded, knowing that another reporter had already been assigned to cover the event at the newspaper.

Tanner frowned. "Really? All day...?"

"Part of the day," she said truthfully.

"So spend the other part at the grand opening. It'll be fun, even for a nongambler."

Bianca didn't doubt that, even if she was sure he'd be far too busy as cohost to even notice her there. "I'll think about it."

"Fair enough," he said evenly.

"You can let me off here," Bianca instructed Johan. He pulled up in front of the Owen-Knight Building. Bianca looked at Tanner. "Thanks for the lift."

"Anytime," he said smoothly. "But hopefully next time it won't be because we ran into your car."

She smiled. "I agree. Speaking of..."

"It may take a few days to get it repaired, but my man will take care of it. If you need a loaner or..."

"I can wait. I'll take a cab until then." She certainly couldn't expect him to shepherd her around. Nor would she want him to. They exchanged contact information. "Bye."

"Till we meet again," Tanner told her, as if it were written in stone.

Bianca wasn't so sure about that. Yes, she was definitely attracted to the man. Who wouldn't be? But that didn't mean she was eager to become another notch on his belt. *That was, if he hadn't already lost count, she thought*

She watched as the limousine drove off. Her thoughts turned to the grand opening gala at Aloha Seas and the opportunity to see Tanner again in his element.

## Chapter 2

"Since when did you start arriving at work in a limo?" Melanie Rice, Bianca's coworker and friend asked.

"Since the limo driver ran into my car," Bianca said as they both went inside the building.

Melanie, who was the same age and a little taller, cast Bianca a doubtful look. "And that's how he's repaying you?"

"Something like that." Bianca suppressed a smile. "The limo actually belongs to Tanner Long."

"*The* Tanner Long?" Melanie asked, her blue eyes widening.

"Unless there's another one I don't know about," Bianca joked.

"There's only one man who looks *that* good," declared Melanie as they entered the elevator. "Maybe two, if you include his brother."

Bianca found it hard to argue the point, but decided to do so anyway. "He's not that great. But Tanner did step up and offer to have my car repaired, free of charge."

"Oh, really?" Melanie pushed a strand of curly dark hair from her face. "How'd you manage that?"

"Wasn't too difficult," Bianca said. "After all, it was his driver who was too close to my car when I had to stop suddenly to avoid hitting someone else."

"Either way, my guess is that you left as much of an impression on Mr. Long as he did on you."

*Did I?* Bianca wondered. *Or would any attractive woman who kept herself in shape have impressed him?*

"I doubt that," she responded. "He was too preoccupied with the grand opening of his hotel-casino to be thinking about leaving impressions."

"We should go to the grand opening," Melanie said as the elevator doors opened to the sixth floor. "I know Oscar Presley has been assigned to write a piece for the paper. But now that you know one of the owners personally—"

Bianca chuckled. "I wouldn't exactly put it that way," she said, then admitted, "But he did invite me."

"Then it's settled," Melanie said, practically jumping for joy, as if they had both won the lottery. "I'm sure he won't mind if I tag along, and maybe I'll even put a few dollars in the slot machines."

"I'm sure he won't mind," Bianca agreed, especially when they would probably fade into the woodwork with all the city's dignitaries on hand to welcome the Aloha Seas to Las Vegas.

Melanie beamed. "Now I just have to decide what to wear. You never know who we might run into."

Knowing that her friend turned heads all the time,

Bianca was certain that would be no problem. "I'm sure we'll both look great no matter what we wear."

"Maybe so," Melanie said. "But there's nothing wrong with a little icing on the cake, so to speak."

Bianca grinned. "Whatever you say." She reached her workstation. "I'll talk to you later."

Sitting at her desk, Bianca attempted to concentrate on a few articles she was working on. If only her thoughts weren't filled with images of Tanner Long.

Tanner walked into the hotel. Everything sparkled, and it was a damned good imitation of Hawaii, complete with palm trees, sand, pool replicas of the ocean, an amazing luau area, and authentic Hawaiian cuisine and drinks. There were two nightclubs and a concert hall. Of course, there was also a casino that was pure Las Vegas with plenty of slot machines, blackjack tables, card dealers and a professional and friendly staff to keep things running smoothly.

He thought about Bianca. Perhaps it was serendipitous that their cars had collided. Otherwise he might never have laid eyes on the beauty. He was a firm believer in fate and that all things happened for a reason.

He liked the idea of getting to know Bianca better. But first, she had to show up for the grand opening. Then they could take it from there, assuming she didn't bring a date. He certainly didn't mind a little competition from time to time. But when it came to women, he preferred not to have to compete for anyone he had his eye on.

And currently that was Bianca Wagner, whom he knew far too little about at the moment. He hoped to rectify that soon.

"There you are…." Tanner heard the familiar voice, breaking his reverie.

He turned to see his brother approaching with Frank Regan, the general manager.

"For a minute there, I thought you'd gone to the wrong place," Solomon said.

"I had to make a slight detour," Tanner explained, gazing at his brother. They were the same height. Many had said they would be hard to tell apart between their close features and size, except Solomon chose to wear his black hair long and curly instead of shaving it all off. Tanner was glad that set them apart. The last thing he needed or wanted was to have people getting him confused with his brother and vice versa. Particularly where it concerned the ladies, as their tastes were about as different as night and day.

"Oh, right, the accident," Solomon said.

"What accident?" Frank asked, scratching his thinning blond-gray hair.

"Just a slight fender bender," Tanner said. "I took care of it. No big deal."

"Glad to hear that," Solomon told him. "We've got less than forty-eight hours till the big opening, and there's still a lot to be done."

Tanner smiled. "Including cost cutting?"

"Hey, someone has to watch the bottom line," his brother said with a chuckle.

"And you're the right man for the job. Don't you agree, Frank?"

"Absolutely," he said. "Together, you two are unbeatable."

"Which makes the three of us that much more formidable," Tanner told him, patting the fiftysomething general manager on the back. They began walking and

Tanner regarded both men. "So bring me up to speed on anything I've missed, and I'll do the same."

"Well, for one, you missed the glamorous Kendre Kelly rehearsing for her opening act in the concert hall," Frank told him.

Tanner frowned. She was one of the top singing talents around these days. They had secured her services for the next three months. He would have more than enough time to see her perform.

"Is she as good as they say?" he asked for effect.

"Better," Frank claimed. "Back me up on this, Solomon."

"Yeah, she's good—including on the eyes."

Tanner chuckled. "Leave it up to my brother to focus more on her looks than talent."

"Look who's talking," Solomon tossed back. "I'm not the one who dated a hot-to-trot dancer, awed much more by her beauty than her footwork."

"Guilty as charged," Tanner said. "But then, she didn't work for me. Have to draw the line somewhere."

Solomon grinned crookedly. "Understood."

Tanner wasn't so sure he did, knowing Solomon had a weakness for beautiful women. The fact that Kendre was now employed at the Aloha Seas would not likely change this any.

For his part, Tanner could also appreciate a lovely, sexy woman. Bianca Wagner came to mind again. Good thing she wasn't working for them, so there were no barriers standing in the way of them getting together, assuming the opportunity presented itself.

Bianca resisted the urge to overdress for the grand opening event, preferring to keep it simple and stylish with a sleeveless blue A-line dress and low heels. She decided to leave her hair down and loose, and wore little makeup, as usual, preferring the natural glow of her complexion.

Accompanied by Melanie, she entered the packed Aloha Seas and both women were immediately in awe.

"This is so cool," Melanie said, taking in the glamor and glitter of the tropical-themed hotel. "Makes me want to check out Hawaii in person."

"You should," Bianca told her. "You'd love it there."

"I'm sure I would, especially with the right man on my arm."

Bianca smiled. "That's always a plus," she said.

"Aloha!" Bianca heard the familiar deep voice. She turned to find Tanner standing there with another tall, well-dressed man who, by the looks of him, could only be Tanner's brother.

"Hello," she said.

Tanner grinned. "Glad you could make it."

"We wouldn't have missed this," Melanie said enthusiastically.

"This is my friend, Melanie," Bianca said.

"Nice to meet you," Tanner told her, shaking Melanie's hand. "And this is my brother, Solomon."

"Ladies," Solomon said, smiling.

Bianca smiled back. She could see the resemblance between the brothers right down to the neatly trimmed mustaches and goatees, aside from the fact that Solomon had hair atop his head and Tanner did not.

"Was your car repaired to your satisfaction?" Tanner asked her.

"It will be ready in two days," Bianca told him. "Thank you."

"It was the least I could do, since Johan caused the damage."

"I really love the hotel," Melanie said.

*"Mahalo!"* Solomon responded, thanking her.

"Can't wait to see the casino."

"I'd be happy to give you a tour," he said.

"I'll take you up on that," Melanie responded, beaming.

Solomon grinned. "Then let's go for it."

Bianca watched as the two walked away, leaving her alone with Tanner. "That was quick," she commented.

"For Melanie or Solomon?" he quipped.

"Both."

Tanner chuckled. "Solomon's always had an eye for pretty ladies. Your friend certainly fits the bill."

Bianca couldn't argue the point. She only hoped Melanie knew what she was getting herself into. Or maybe Melanie didn't care. Bianca was well aware that her friend was a free spirit, often living for the moment rather than the future.

"Why don't I show you around," Tanner said loudly, amidst an exquisite setting overflowing with invited guests, tourists and employees moving this way and that with blended chatter. "If you'd like?"

"Are you sure I wouldn't be keeping you from anything?" she asked tentatively.

"I've got a lot on my plate today," he admitted. "But I think I can spare a few minutes for a beautiful lady."

Bianca warmed to the compliment, even though she suspected he used that line quite a bit on women. "Okay, in that case, I'll take a few minutes of your time to check out the place."

Tanner flashed a pleased smile. "I like your dress."

"It's just a dress," she said, trying to downplay it.

"Not on you," he insisted.

She laughed. "Are you always this smooth?"

He chuckled. "It's not a line, I assure you. I always say just what I mean."

"Then, thank you," Bianca gave in, figuring she would accept the flattery since she could just as easily have complimented him on the designer clothing that seemed made just for him.

Tanner flashed another devastatingly handsome smile and proffered his long arm, pointing toward an enormous lobby. "Shall we...?"

Tanner was only too happy to give Bianca a tour of his pride and joy. He knew Solomon felt the same way when showing Melanie around. Though this hardly meant either of them was expecting more, Tanner would not deny that he was attracted to Bianca, and he sensed she was attracted to him, too. How far they would take that was anyone's guess, but he was more than happy to see if it could go anywhere.

"Wow!" Bianca marveled as he showed her one of the pools that had the feel of being on Maui's famed Kaanapali Beach, complete with palm trees, golden sand and plenty of sunshine.

"You like?" Tanner asked.

"I love it!"

"I take it you swim?"

"Of course," she said.

"Then feel free to drop in sometime for a dip. The water's always comfortable."

Bianca looked at him. "Have you tested it?"

He chuckled. "Yeah, I've been in a couple of times to break it in, so to speak."

"Maybe I'll take you up on that sometime."

"I hope so." *And I just might join you in the water*

*for some real fun,* he thought. "Let's go look at the lounges."

"Sounds good."

Tanner ordered them each a Mai Tai in the Island Lounge. "So what do you do for a living?"

"I'm a writer," Bianca responded.

"You write novels, articles or—"

"Yes, articles for the *Vegas Valley Happenings* and some freelance stuff for online publications."

"Cool," he said, picturing her at work on her next article.

"Not as cool as owning your own hotel-casino," she said flatly.

He chuckled. "It definitely has its perks and advantages, but that's only a part of who I am."

"And just who are you?" Bianca asked as she sipped her drink.

"I'm someone with a wide range of tastes and experiences."

"Oh, really?"

"Yeah."

"Such as…" she asked.

He was about to answer when his cell phone rang. It was Frank.

"I have to get this," Tanner said reluctantly.

"Of course," Bianca said.

He stood up and took the call, listening as Frank informed him that he had a welcoming speech to make in fifteen minutes.

"I'll be there," Tanner said. He gazed at Bianca, feeling that he could look at her all day and night. If only he had the time. "I hate to cut this short, but I have to play host in welcoming some dignitaries to the grand opening."

"I understand." She gave him a polite smile.

"Can you hang around for a while?" he asked hope-fully.

"Maybe," she said hesitantly.

He grinned. "Good. I'd like to finish what we started. In the meantime, have another drink on the house."

Bianca tilted her head. "You're not trying to get me drunk, are you?"

Tanner chuckled. "No, I'd much rather have you clear-headed. It's sexier."

"So you think I'm sexy?"

He saw no reason to deny it. "Not think. I know you are," he said. "Well, I'll leave you with that thought."

Tanner walked away from the bar, hoping this might be the start of something good for both of them.

# Chapter 3

That night, Bianca sat in a bubble bath, shamelessly fantasizing about Tanner Long. In spite of the definite sexual vibes between them, she wasn't holding her breath that anything would actually come of it. She wasn't the type of woman to just jump into bed with any man she was attracted to. Especially a wealthy man with a reputation for loving and leaving women.

She hadn't exactly gone out of her way to become involved with anyone at this time in her life. And she sensed the same was true for Tanner. No involvement of a serious nature.

*So where does that leave us as potential lovers?* she asked herself, using her toes to toss bubbles in the air. Probably nowhere, which was probably the safest place.

Bianca thought back to being at the Aloha Seas in a very nice lounge after Tanner had left. She had quickly grown bored and gone to find him. She did, in a huge ballroom filled with people. Standing tall at a podium, Tanner had seemed totally in his element. Flanked by gorgeous showgirls, he'd welcomed the mayor and other dignitaries while promising a bright future for the city of Las Vegas and Aloha Seas as a new addition to the Strip.

She had left the hotel before he had finished entertaining his guests, figuring that was probably best all the way around.

Melanie had left with her, but not before making plans for a date with Solomon. Bianca had a feeling that any romance between them would be short-lived, if Solomon's reputation was even close to the truth. The same feeling about Tanner left her less than enthusiastic about any future with him, should the possibility present itself.

The next day at work, all Melanie could talk about was Solomon.

"He's such a hunk, and he likes me," she gushed.

"He likes all attractive women," Bianca reminded her.

"And I like all good-looking men," Melanie countered. "Doesn't mean I'll sleep with every one of them."

"I never said that."

"You also never told me if you plan to see Tanner again."

"Not if I can help it," Bianca said, wondering if it was as simple as that.

"Give the man a chance," Melanie said. "I saw the way he was looking at you. In fact, he couldn't take his eyes off you."

Bianca smiled diffidently. "I wouldn't go that far."

"Well, maybe you should. He's a hottie, loaded and

looks to be in the market for a special lady—someone like you. Don't blow it by playing too hard to get."

"I don't play games with men." Unlike some other women she knew. "I'm just not looking to go there right now. Okay?"

"Okay, I get it." Melanie sighed. "Not interested. Doesn't mean we can't go to their casino together sometimes for drinks or whatever. As huge as the place is, chances are you'd never run into Tanner."

"Sure, no problem," Bianca said. Somehow she was sure that any time she set foot in the Aloha Seas, she would invariably run into Tanner.

Tanner worked out on the elliptical machine in the hotel's state-of-the-art fitness room alongside his brother. They were in regular competition over who was the fittest. In Tanner's mind it was probably a tie, even though he'd never admit to it.

He thought about Bianca. After standing at the podium yesterday, thanking everyone who had made it possible for the hotel and casino to come about, he had gone to look for Bianca. But she was nowhere to be found.

Though disappointed, Tanner had given her the benefit of the doubt in her absence. Maybe she got tired of waiting and had other things to do. Should he call her? Did she want him to?

Or was he interested in someone who wasn't able or ready to reciprocate that interest?

*Maybe it's best if I don't rush into anything for a change,* he mused, *only to end up feeling empty and ready to move on.*

Tanner had a feeling that this wouldn't be the case

with Bianca. But he might never get the chance to find out.

"So what's up with you and Bianca?" Solomon asked, as if reading his mind.

"Not much," Tanner admitted. "She left before we could spend any time together."

"But you like her, right?"

"I'm attracted to her, yes." Tanner increased his speed on the machine. "Can't say yet if I like her."

"Maybe you should find out," Solomon said, wiping perspiration from his brow. "She's definitely got the looks."

"So does Melanie," Tanner said, eyeing him. "You two seemed to hit it off."

"Yeah, we did. We're going out tonight."

"Lucky you—or is she the lucky one?"

Solomon laughed. "Hey, we're in the business of luck, right? We'll see what happens. In the meantime, maybe you ought to give Bianca a buzz and take it from there. Or are you still hung up on…what's her name…"

"That's over and done with," Tanner interjected before his brother could finish.

"Thought so. Just checking."

"Well, check no further," Tanner told him, eager to distance himself from Angie LeBrock, an aspiring actress and singer he'd hooked up with a few times. While it had been fun for a while, she soon became too overbearing and clingy for his liking.

He was now ready to move on.

Bianca had just left work and was heading toward her car when her cell phone rang. She pulled the phone from her purse and saw from the caller ID that it was

Tanner Long. Her heart skipped a beat as she thought about him.

"Hello," she said equably, just before her voice mail picked up.

"Hey, this is Tanner," he said curtly. "You weren't around last night to pick up where we left off."

"Sorry, I had things to do. And, clearly, you were pretty busy, so…"

"Yeah, guess it was kind of crazy around here," Tanner conceded. "You have any plans for tonight?"

She sucked in a breath. "Are you asking me out on a date?"

"Yes. One of our restaurants specializes in seafood, if that suits your fancy."

"I love seafood," she admitted.

"Great. So what do you say?"

Bianca considered the invitation. Did she really want to head in this direction with this man? She hesitated. "Actually, I'm busy tonight."

"So how about tomorrow night?" Tanner persisted.

"Why me?" she asked bluntly. "Don't you have enough showgirls and others to choose from to go out with?"

He chuckled. "First, you're a beautiful woman and I would like to get to know you. Second, I don't date showgirls. As for others, sure there are plenty of lovely ladies in Vegas to ask out, but I'm asking *you*."

Bianca admired his honesty and, even if she was leery, couldn't resist her attraction to him. "All right— tomorrow night."

"I'll have Johan pick you up."

"Oh, no." She laughed nervously. "I don't know if I can trust him behind the wheel. I think I'm better off taking a cab there." Her car was still being serviced.

Tanner seemed to take it all in stride. "Whatever you like. But, just for the record, Johan can only work with what he's given, as far as reaction time goes."

Bianca furrowed her brow. "Sounds like you're blaming me for what happened."

"I'm blaming the idiot who cut you off," he said bluntly. "The important thing is that no one got hurt."

"True," Bianca agreed, glad they were on the same wavelength. Though Johan may not have been at fault, in reality, she didn't want to be in an awkward situation on a first date, just in case it went totally the wrong way and she wanted to cut it short.

Still, she was optimistic that the date could turn out to be a good thing. After all, there was no denying that Tanner was a good catch.

That night, Bianca stuck with her original plans to meet her good friend, Vicky Poole, for drinks at a club on Paradise Road called The Palace.

She had known Vicky for a few years now—they met when Bianca was a crime reporter. Vicky, an ex-prostitute, had turned her life around and was counseling teen runaways and sex workers, getting them off the street. She now ran a safe house for prostitute girls.

"Hey there," Vicky said, waving as she made her way through the crowd to reach Bianca.

"Hey," Bianca responded with a smile, giving the taller, slender woman a hug. "I got us a table."

"Cool." Vicky put her oversize purse on the table and sat across from Bianca. They both ordered cocktails when the waitress approached.

"How's the safe house?" Bianca asked, knowing how important this was to Vicky. Bianca volunteered there once every two weeks.

"It can be utterly exhausting at times," Vicky responded, running a hand through her short brown hair with its golden highlights. "But I love being there for the girls, you know?"

"I know," Bianca said. "And they love having you there, knowing someone cares."

"Yeah, I do. I only wish someone had been there to care for me when I worked the Strip as a teenager."

Bianca couldn't begin to imagine the hell Vicky must have endured at that stage of her life. She reached across the table and touched Vicky's hand. "The important thing is that you got through it in one piece and are doing good things with your life now."

"Very true," she said.

The drinks came and Bianca sipped hers thoughtfully.

"So bring me up-to-date on what's going on with you," Vicky said.

*Should I or shouldn't I mention Tanner?* Bianca asked herself. After all, they hadn't even gone on a date yet. She also wondered if she might jinx any potential they had by jumping the gun.

Then she realized that if it was meant to go somewhere it would. And if not, it wouldn't.

"Well, I met Tanner Long," Bianca said casually, knowing that he was well-known to most women in the city, thanks to his most-eligible-bachelor tag.

"Get out of here," Vicky said in disbelief. "Or do you mean you met him as a reporter?"

"Actually, I met him as a car owner."

Vicky cocked a brow. "Explain."

"His limo driver hit my car and I ended up getting a ride from Tanner," Bianca said nonchalantly. "Next thing I knew, he invited me to the grand opening of his hotel and casino. He asked me out to dinner tomorrow night."

"Whoa—this is in warp speed!" Vicky said. "How on earth did you get from point A to point, let's say, N or O…?"

Bianca giggled. "It just happened. Well, nothing's really happened yet, but he seems to like me, so we'll see where it goes, if anywhere."

"Well you go, girl!" Vicky lifted her hand and gave Bianca a high five. "After being with too many losers, maybe you've finally met your match. Or should I say it's the other way around?"

"Maybe a little of both," Bianca said. "But it's way too early to think about matches made in heaven. After all, this is Sin City, is it not?"

Vicky laughed. "It is, but that doesn't mean there aren't still good people around with good intentions."

"Tanner seems to have good intentions with Aloha Seas as a new place of employment on the Strip," Bianca told her. "Not so sure what his intentions are as a confirmed playboy."

"Hey, being a player usually only means the man hasn't met anyone yet to get him to slow down. Could be you're just the right person for the job."

Bianca chuckled. "This isn't an interview. Just a first date."

"So enjoy, and see what the man is made of—besides millions."

"I intend to," Bianca said. She was in no way a gold digger—she was more than happy to support herself. But she did want a man who was self-assured, successful and wasn't into head games. Or leading her on just because he could. Could Tanner be that man?

Or was she setting herself up for yet another disappointment?

# Chapter 4

After a brisk morning workout, Tanner had showered in his penthouse suite and then attended a series of meetings with his management team. So far, so good for the hotel-casino. They had gotten a lot of press coverage. But he understood that they were in competition with every other hotel and casino on the Strip, as well as those off it. As such, they had to be innovative and welcoming if they were going to stay ahead of the game.

After the meeting ended, Tanner had hoped to talk to Solomon alone, but he was meeting Melanie for lunch—apparently in his room where she had spent the night. Admittedly, Tanner was envious of his little brother. He had sought out the prize and conquered with seemingly little effort on his part.

Whereas Tanner felt as though he was starting from scratch with Bianca. She didn't strike him as the kind of woman who would settle for a one-night stand. Especially not the first night. And though he had been guilty of that a time or two, the truth was he preferred a steady relationship, contrary to popular belief. Finding a woman who could hold his attention was key.

Bianca certainly seemed like a good candidate.

After doing some paperwork, Tanner went to the hotel's Mahalo Lounge to have a drink with his best friend and lawyer, Chuck Newman. Aside from the fact that they had known each other for more than a decade, Chuck was also one of the hotel-casino's investors and someone he could trust to tell it like it was.

Tanner spotted him nursing a drink at the bar.

"Hope you haven't had too many of those yet," Tanner kidded.

Chuck looked up and grinned. "This is my first one."

Tanner smiled, sitting next to the thirty-eight-year-old man. "In that case, I'll order a second round for you and one for myself."

"That works for me," Chuck said. His short black hair was graying at the temples.

Tanner ordered the drinks from the bartender who promptly made them.

"Looks like this place has set the Strip on fire," Chuck commented.

"Yeah, all the rooms are booked for the next couple of weeks and some high rollers have shown up hoping to get lucky."

Chuck laughed. "That always helps. Unless, of course, you're pulling for the house, which I am."

Tanner chuckled. "You had me worried for a moment there," he joked.

"Don't be. I want to see my investment grow tenfold, if possible."

"You and me both." Tanner tasted the drink. "So how's Deloris?" he asked about Chuck's wife.

"Great. She's in South Carolina visiting her mother." Chuck looked at him. "And who's the flavor of the week for you right now?"

Tanner laughed. "Sounds like ice cream."

"Only sweeter, potentially," Chuck shot back.

"I'm not seeing anyone right now," Tanner told him.

"No…? Losing your touch, friend?"

"Been too preoccupied of late." Tanner thought of Bianca. "Actually, I do have a date tonight."

Chuck smiled. "Figured you wouldn't go too long without having someone on your arm. I suppose she's gorgeous?"

"Yeah, she is," Tanner admitted.

"Why am I not surprised? Between you and your brother, you pretty much have the run of the best ladies in town."

Tanner grinned. "I wish," he said lightly. "Truth of the matter is both of us really just want someone we can grow old with and still be madly in love. Until that person comes along, all we can do is keep looking."

"Then here's to looking and finding that right lady," Chuck said, lifting his glass. "Assuming you haven't already…"

Tanner took that toast and sipped his drink, his thoughts squarely on Bianca and their date tonight.

After paying the cabdriver, Bianca headed into the Aloha Seas. She was feeling a little nervous, as though this were a high school date instead of an evening with a handsome, millionaire playboy on his own turf.

*You'll be fine,* she told herself. *Just keep the expectations low and the optimism high.*

She had barely stepped onto the marble floor in the lobby, when Bianca saw Tanner approaching with a big smile on his face.

"Right on time," he said.

"I could say the same for you," she told him, in spite of the fact that he had the advantage of already being there ahead of time.

"I'd never be late for dinner with you."

"Oh, really?" Bianca wasn't sure if he was the consummate charmer. Or simply full of it. She preferred the former.

"Not when you look like that," Tanner said, giving her the once-over.

Bianca colored as he admired her in a red scoop-neck top, black skirt and black pumps. She studied him in a gray blazer, dusty pink polo shirt and gray slacks before declaring, "You're not so bad yourself."

He laughed. "Thanks. I wanted to at least make myself presentable for the occasion."

She doubted he'd ever have a problem when it came to style and taste, imagining he wore expensive attire regularly.

"So show me this great seafood restaurant," she said.

Tanner grinned. "It would be my pleasure."

They entered Seas and were led to a private table.

"Your very own table," Bianca said as he pulled out her seat. "Impressive."

"One of the bonuses of being majority owner," he said coolly.

"Must be nice," she teased as he sat.

"It's much nicer to have you as my guest."

She smiled while thinking, *anytime*. But that wouldn't be true, as she wanted more from a man than a great table at a restaurant. Or, for that matter, a very handsome man as her companion. But both were a good start.

A waiter came over and handed them menus. "Can I get you something to drink, Mr. Long? Or Ms....?"

"Bianca," she said, adding, "red wine, please."

"Same," Tanner said.

"Red wine, it is," the waiter responded. "I'll be back to take your order shortly."

"So, what do you recommend?" Bianca asked.

Tanner regarded the menu. "I've only dined here once thus far, and I found the stuffed-shrimp dish with walnut-blended greens to be first rate."

"Sounds good," she said. "I'll try it."

"I'll join you," he told her.

A few minutes later, they were sipping their wine.

"Let's get back to the wide range of tastes and experiences you were going to tell me about the other day," Bianca said, eager to see all sides of the man.

"Thought you'd never ask," Tanner said over the rim of his goblet with a chuckle. "Well, let's see, I like to work out—including tennis, bicycling, jogging, basketball, swimming and hitting the gym. I'm big on traveling—mostly for business, but pleasure as well."

"Where have you traveled?" she wondered, speculating that he had been all over the world.

"Lots of places, both in the U.S. and abroad. I've been to Hawaii a number of times, which gave me the inspiration for the theme of Aloha Seas. I've also been to Europe, Australia and, closer to home, Canada—Toronto and Montreal."

"Looks like you've built up a lot of frequent flier miles," Bianca half joked.

"Yeah, you could say that." Tanner wet his lips with

wine. "I have my own jet now, so the rewards of flying often are always there."

"I'll bet." While she had met some people in the entertainment business who had private planes, Bianca had never known anyone personally who owned a jet. What other things would she learn about him?

"Getting back to my tastes, I enjoy professional sports such as basketball, football, baseball and boxing, reading the classics and contemporary mysteries and thrillers, watching music performances and plays, and, believe it or not, doing crossword puzzles."

Bianca laughed. "That is quite a range." *And one I'd have a hard time topping,* she mused.

"I also do my share of charity work, both locally and nationally," Tanner said.

"Nice to hear." She smiled at him, while thinking that he was certainly well-rounded and humble. Those were good qualities to have.

The food came and she watched Tanner dive right in. She did the same, as their wineglasses were refilled.

"Your turn," he said, dabbing a cloth napkin to the corners of his mouth.

Bianca had expected this, but never really liked talking too much about herself. "What would you like to know?" she asked cautiously.

"What wouldn't I like to know is more like it." Tanner flashed her a serious look. "Have you ever been married?"

"No."

"How about engaged?"

She smiled. "Not that, either."

"But you've had boyfriends?"

"Of course," she said. "I just haven't found the right guy to get engaged to or marry yet."

"So, no children, then?" Tanner asked levelly.

Bianca gave a little laugh, feeling as though she was being interviewed as wife material. Was that so bad? Or was it a bit too personal for a first date?

"No, I don't have any children," she told him. "Do you?"

"Nope," he answered concisely.

"Do you want any?" Bianca had to ask for some reason.

Tanner sighed. "Someday. I'm not in any hurry, though."

"Neither am I." She wanted to make this clear, preferring to leave all the mommying to her sister for now.

He seemed content with her answer and resumed eating. "Tell me about your family. I know you said you're from Houston. Fill in some blanks."

She put down her fork. "Well, my parents are divorced. My dad lives in Biloxi and Mom in Galveston."

"I lost my folks some time back," he said sadly. "Dad from a heart attack, Mom from cancer."

Bianca cringed on hearing this. "I'm so sorry about your parents."

Tanner raised his chin. "So am I. But they had a good life for as long as it lasted."

Bianca was glad that he seemed to have come to terms with their passing. She wondered how long it would take her to do the same when her parents passed away. "I have a sister who lives in Portland, Oregon," she told him, "with her husband and his twin daughters."

"Portland, huh?" Tanner leaned forward interestedly. "I've been there a couple of times, as well as Seattle."

"The Pacific Northwest is a great place to visit," Bianca told him.

"Aside from Texas and Oregon, where else have you been?" he asked curiously.

"Can't say I can match your travels, but I've been here and there."

"Such as…"

"Let's see…most of the midwestern and western states, New York, Atlanta, New Orleans Miami, Seattle and Honolulu twice." She paused to collect her thoughts. "Abroad, I've been to Brazil, Canada, the Cayman Islands, England, Mexico and Sweden."

"Not bad," Tanner said, slicing through his shrimp stuffed with crab and cheddar cheese. "So what do you do for sport? It's obvious you keep yourself in great shape."

"Thank you," Bianca told him, happy that he noticed. "I jog almost daily."

"Cool. Maybe we can run together sometime."

"Sounds good to me." She imagined seeing him in a T-shirt and shorts, showing off his well-defined, muscular limbs.

"Then we'll make it happen." Tanner lifted his glass. "What type of music are you into? I'm guessing pop and R&B, maybe a little jazz, cabaret and blues. How am I doing?"

Bianca laughed. "Not too bad. You can probably scratch the blues off the list, though it was my dad's favorite type of music. But I'm definitely into R&B, pop and jazz. I love Alicia Keys, Adele, Bruno Mars, Kendre Kelly, Rihanna and Michael Bublé, among many others."

"Yeah, I like them, too. Seems like we have a few things in common."

"Seems that way," she agreed, tasting the greens. "But I have to admit, I haven't done any crossword puzzles in a while and generally prefer literary and romance novels to mysteries and thrillers."

Tanner chuckled. "I could see that. Guess I'll have to work on you with the crossword puzzles."

"Oh, you think so?"

"Yeah, it could be fun trying to solve the mystery together."

"Maybe," she said, wondering what other common ground they might find. She watched his lips move sexily as he chewed. "So are you a self-made millionaire? Or did you get where you are through inherited wealth?"

*Hope I'm not being too nosey,* Bianca told herself. But she was curious and he seemed comfortable enough in his own skin to talk about almost anything.

"A bit of both," Tanner revealed. "My father was a wealthy real-estate investor, among other ventures. While Solomon and I benefited from this, much of what my parents earned was donated to charity, as they wanted us to succeed on our own to a large degree. And we have, turning a small fortune into a large one."

"That's impressive." She applauded him. "Obviously you've invested your money wisely."

"Yeah, it's worked out well so far, but I'm not taking anything for granted. I don't expect to just sit on my butt and rake in the dough. I'm all about rolling up my sleeves and working as hard as any of my employees to keep the sense of accomplishment and satisfaction in what I do."

"Looks like you are very grounded," Bianca said.

"I could say the same for you." Tanner met her eyes in earnest. "Guess we're cut from the same cloth."

She chuckled. "Maybe not quite."

His thick brows lowered. "Why do you say that?"

*Should I go there and possibly ruin the mood?*

Bianca asked herself. "Well, if I'm not mistaken, you've built quite a reputation for yourself as one of the most eligible bachelors in the city. It seems like you're not very interested in settling down with just one woman."

Tanner tasted the wine. "As a writer, you shouldn't believe everything you read or hear."

Her eyes widened defensively. "Are you denying it?"

"I admit to never marrying and being in the company of single women from time to time. But that doesn't mean I'm just a player and not looking for that one special lady."

"So you are looking for that special lady?" Bianca asked bluntly, hoping it didn't sound as though she were volunteering for the job.

"Yeah, I am," Tanner said without preface. "And are you looking for that one special guy?"

"Of course," she responded truthfully and then decided to tone this down, so there was no pressure either way. "But I'm in no hurry. When it happens, it happens. Until then, I'm just happy to be with some pleasant company."

He grinned. "Touché."

After the meal, which Tanner felt ended too soon, he walked Bianca outside. It was a warm night. He would like nothing better than to take her to his suite and make love to her. But it was obvious that she was not interested in a casual fling. Neither was he, where she was concerned.

"Are you sure I can't have Johan give you a lift home?" Tanner asked. It would give him the opportunity to go along for the ride.

"Thanks, but I'll stick with the cab," Bianca told him.

He accepted her choice, while hoping this would

change in the future. He got her a taxi, then Tanner opened the door for Bianca. He badly wanted to kiss her. Something told him she wanted the same. Or was that merely his fantasy?

Going with his instincts, Tanner lifted her chin and gazed into Bianca's eyes for a long moment before tilting his head and planting a kiss on her lips. They were, as expected, soft and perfect when meshing with his. He kept the kiss going for several seconds and then pulled back, not wanting to overdo it.

"That was nice," Bianca uttered.

"Yeah, for me too," he assured her.

"Good night, Tanner."

"Good night."

He smiled and watched her slide into the backseat before he closed the door.

As the cab drove off, Tanner watched for a moment, wishing he'd gone with her. She'd left quite an impression on him—one that he did not take lightly.

*Bianca Wagner may be just the lady I've been looking for all my adult life,* he thought. But the trick was getting her to feel the same way about him. He would work on that and not allow this gorgeous woman to slip through his fingers.

Tanner went back inside the hotel and made the rounds, greeting guests warmly, even while his thoughts were decidedly on Bianca.

## Chapter 5

The following morning, Tanner joined Solomon in the Tiki Room for breakfast. There were waffles and sausage links already on the table.

"You look tired," Tanner said, taking a seat opposite his brother. "It must have been a tough night."

"I wouldn't exactly call it tough," Solomon said, sipping coffee. "Melanie kept me going and going and—"

"I get the picture." Tanner lifted up a hand to halt him. "Glad to see you two have clicked for however long that might be." He knew his brother had a habit of moving through ladies faster than he got rid of clothes.

"I'm not looking too far ahead," Solomon told him. "Right now, I'm just enjoying her company."

"And clearly she's enjoying yours, too," Tanner teased him.

Solomon dug his fork into the waffle. "How did it go with you and Bianca last night?"

"It was good." Tanner stirred his coffee. "I like her."

"So tell me something I don't know. But is she any good in bed?"

"We haven't gotten that far," admitted Tanner.

"Holding back on you, is she?"

"We're holding back on each other. I don't want to rush things with her."

"That's a switch," Solomon said. "Growing soft on Bianca before you even sample the merchandise?"

Tanner frowned. "She's a classy lady, and I'd rather not screw things up by making it seem like all I'm interested in is getting her into bed."

Solomon cocked a brow. "So, what are you looking for here—someone to marry and settle down with?"

"No, I simply want someone I can relate to and who can hold my interest in and out of bed. You should try it sometime. You might like it."

"I'll keep that in mind," Solomon said. "But I'm in no hurry to take that path. Maybe you're not, either."

"We'll see about that," Tanner said, feeling he was more than ready to leave the playboy life behind and start a real relationship. But was Bianca ready to take that journey with him?

His cell phone rang, and for an instant Tanner thought it might be Bianca. But the caller ID showed it was Angie LeBrock, the last person he wanted to talk to. He'd been avoiding her calls because she didn't seem to take no for an answer when he told her things were over between them. Apart from not having much of a personality, frankly, she seemed more interested in what he had than who he was.

He ignored the call.

Solomon noticed. "Who was that?"

Tanner frowned. "Angie."

"Thought you ended things with her."

"So did I," Tanner said glumly. "She thinks otherwise."

"Is she stalking you now?" Solomon asked.

"I wouldn't say that, but she is being somewhat of a pest," Tanner said.

"So call her back and tell her to lay off."

"That would probably only encourage her into believing there was still a chance for us to get back together." He didn't want to make this any more difficult than necessary.

Tanner then considered how much better off he could be with Bianca in his life, as they seemed to hit it off. Was she feeling the same way?

On Saturday, Bianca dropped by Melanie's town house after finishing her laundry and other household chores. Her friend was bubbly.

"Solomon and I are going to check out Cirque du Soleil tonight," gushed Melanie over tea as they sat in her breakfast room.

"Looks like things are really starting to click with you two," Bianca said enviously.

"Just a little." Melanie giggled. "Well…a *lot* in the bedroom. They man is insatiable and seems to know everything it takes to please a woman."

Bianca colored. "Spare me the details, please."

"I'm just saying…" Melanie bit into a piece of toast. "I'm so glad you met Tanner, which led to me meeting Solomon. I have no idea where this is headed, but I'm certainly enjoying the ride."

"I'm happy for you," Bianca said, and meant it. She only hoped Melanie wasn't setting herself up for a fall.

Solomon's reputation as a ladies' man was probably worse than Tanner's.

"Thanks," Melanie said. "I'm happy for you, too."

"We're not exactly where you are in our relationship, if you would even call it that," Bianca pointed out.

"That's not a bad thing," Melanie said. "It doesn't mean you and Tanner aren't of the same mind."

"I know. He seems to respect me and appreciate what I bring to the table, apart from expectations of what I may offer in the bedroom."

"And just wait till he sees that," joked Melanie. "You'll definitely have him in your hip pocket then."

Bianca laughed self-consciously. "We'll see what happens. First, we need a second date. Do you think I should call him?"

"You could," Melanie said, sipping tea. "But I'm sure he'll call you if you don't call him."

Bianca thought about it. She didn't want to blow it with Tanner. She also didn't want to seem too desperate to be with him, although she just really enjoyed his company.

"I'll wait till he calls," she decided.

Melanie smiled. "I know you won't be disappointed."

Bianca sensed she would not be, but still felt a little tense.

That night, Bianca's phone rang, causing her heart to beat a bit faster, thinking it might be Tanner. It was, which brought a smile to her face.

"Hello," she said coolly.

"Hey."

"And how are you?"

"I'm good," he said.

"I'm sure the hotel-casino is keeping you busy," she commented.

"Not too busy to find some time for you. I was wondering if you'd like to go on a walking gourmet-food tour tomorrow afternoon."

"I'd love to," Bianca said. She'd done it once before and had enjoyed it. She knew it would be even better with Tanner's company.

"Wonderful. I hope I can have my driver pick you up and bring you to the hotel. Or if you insist, you can meet me there."

"Hmm…" Bianca thought about it and realized it was silly to blame Johan for hitting her car when it was hardly his fault. "I think I'll be fine having your driver pick me up."

"Cool. Just be sure to save a lot of room in your stomach," Tanner said. "There's a lot to sample."

She laughed. "Of course, but I have to show moderation to maintain my figure."

"Understood and agreed," he said. "Guess we'll both have to pick and choose carefully while enjoying the experience at the same time."

"I'm sure we will," Bianca said, already looking forward to it.

They spoke for only a few more minutes and then Tanner had to cut it short as he was taking a break from a business meeting.

Bianca very much appreciated the gesture and that he cared enough to clear space in his schedule for her. She welcomed the opportunity to get closer.

When the limousine arrived at her house the next day, Bianca was ready. It was another warm afternoon, so she dressed lightly for the outdoor event in a purple short-sleeved V-neck top, white Bermuda shorts and wedge sandals.

Johan opened the back door for her.

"Thanks," she said.

"My pleasure."

Inside, she sat by her lonesome, wishing Tanner was there beside her. She decided to use the time without him to pick Johan's brain about his boss.

"So, what can you tell me about Tanner?" she asked.

He looked at her through the rearview mirror. "Probably a lot. What would you like to know?"

*Actually, everything and anything*, Bianca thought, but doubted he would go that far in telling what he knew. So she tried to keep it basic.

"Does he send you all over the city doing errands for him?"

Johan chuckled. "Yeah, sometimes. No complaints, though. He pays me well to be a driver."

"Have you picked up many ladies for him?" she asked curiously.

"Now you're trying to get me into trouble," he joked.

"I won't say anything if you don't."

"Well, let's just say that he does enjoy female companionship. But Mr. Long is still particular about who he asks out."

Bianca flapped her lashes teasingly. "Oh, is he now…?"

"Yeah, and he likes you," Johan said flatly.

"I like him, too."

"In that case, I hope to see a lot more of you."

She smiled. "Maybe you will."

When he dropped her off in front of the Aloha Seas, Bianca saw Johan make a call on his cell phone as he was driving off. No doubt informing Tanner that she was there.

A tap on her shoulder gave Bianca a start. She turned to see Tanner standing there, putting his cell phone away.

"I see you made it safe and sound," he said smoothly.

"Yes, I did—thanks to Johan."

"Good to know I can count on him to pick you up and bring you here in one piece."

She chuckled, imagining that they could always joke about Johan hitting her car. "He's a good driver," she said, "and obviously devoted to you."

"As I am to him—and you," stressed Tanner.

"Are you?" Bianca gazed up at his face after taking a quick glance at him dressed in a maroon short-sleeved shirt, dark blue pants and sneakers.

"Yes, devoted to seeing where things can go between us."

Her eyes crinkled beneath her sunglasses. "I'd like that, too."

He grinned handsomely. "So let's take our walking tour and see what they have to offer us today."

"I can hardly wait," she said with pure excitement.


"You look nice, by the way," Tanner said, admiring Bianca's long and shapely legs.

"Thank you," she said. "So do you."

He flashed a smile. It was always good for him to hear that his workouts had the effect of keeping him fit and appealing to women. It meant even more when the woman appealed to him.

They stepped inside the Town Square, an outdoor shopping center evocative of a European village.

"Where shall we start?" Tanner asked, taking Bianca's hand.

"Let's see…" she said, squeezing her fingers around his. "How about the Italian café?"

"Sounds good to me."

After sampling the delicacies there, they moved on to an English bistro, then tried some Michoacán treats and onto Caribbean bites—feeding each other from time to time.

"What do you think?" Tanner asked after spoon-feeding Bianca some German ice cream.

She licked her lips. "Very tasty."

"I agree." He smiled. "We'll have to do this again sometime."

"I'd like that, but I have to ask…do you take every girl you like on this walking gourmet tour?"

Tanner met her eyes. "Fair question. But the answer is no. In fact, I have never taken anyone on one of these before. I usually prefer to do my own cooking."

Her lashes fluttered. "So you cook, too?"

"Yep, afraid so."

"No reason to apologize," she stressed softly. "It's terrific when a man can cook."

"I feel the same way about a woman who can cook," he told her. "Not all women do."

"True." She looked at him. "If you're wondering if I can cook, the answer is yes."

He beamed. "Good. I was hoping you'd say that."

"Guess we'll have to put each other to the test."

"How about right now?" Tanner challenged her.

Bianca raised a brow. "You want to cook *now*?"

"No, but I'd like to do this…" He cupped her chin and lifted it before lowering his face. Their mouths pressed together, slightly open, for what Tanner felt was the perfect kiss.

When he pulled away, Bianca touched her lips. "Into public affection, are you?"

"I'm into you," he answered truthfully.

"I'm into you, too," she murmured.

"Why don't we get out of here?" Tanner suggested.

"And go where?"

"How about your place?" Johan had already described her house to him, but Tanner wanted to see it for himself. And more.

"Why don't we let things cool down and do that another time," Bianca suggested.

Tanner wanted her in the worst way and admittedly usually got what he wanted sooner than later. But in this case, making him wait made the slow torture that much more pleasurable.

"I can live with that," he told her. "I'll call Johan and we'll drive you home."

Less than twenty minutes later, Johan drove up to Bianca's house. "Well, here we are," she said.

Tanner gazed at the Spanish home and liked what he saw. He imagined the inside would be even nicer.

"Sure I can't come in for a nightcap?" he asked.

"It's not nighttime," she said jokingly.

"How about an afternoon cap then?"

Bianca smiled. "Hold that thought till the next time."

"I will," Tanner said, eager to spend some time alone with her.

She leaned toward him and gave him a mouthwatering kiss. He put his arms around her, savoring every bit of it while all but ignoring Johan sitting patiently in the driver's seat.

When the kiss ended, Bianca said sweetly, "See you later."

"You can bet on that—even for a nongambler," Tanner assured her.

She smiled. "So can you."

His eyes crinkled and he watched as she got out, closed the car door and headed inside.

Tanner was aroused at the prospect of their being together, even as he willed himself to remain patient for this special lady.

## Chapter 6

Once inside her house, Bianca leaned against the front door. She got a tingly feeling as she replayed the kiss between her and Tanner in her mind. It was just right. *The man knows how to kiss,* she thought. She didn't doubt that he would be just as good a lover, if not even more passionate.

But she'd used her willpower to refrain from inviting him in and allowing their obvious sexual chemistry to take over. Making him wait a little longer would show that she wanted more from him than just sex. She hoped he wanted more than that from her, too.

He seemed to respect that and was patient as they evolved into what she hoped would be a relationship, even if not necessarily a commitment, per se. Not that she was opposed to that. She was simply guarded against the letdown, especially from someone so rich and powerful. He probably had too much on his plate to even look for anything long-term.

*I'll just have to hedge my bets that we do have the makings of something wonderful here, whatever that may be,* Bianca told herself.

After spending a couple of hours on her computer working on an article, she poured herself a glass of wine and called her sister for a video chat.

Madison accepted the call, and her face appeared on Bianca's iPad. "Hey."

"Hi," Bianca said. "Hope I didn't catch you at a bad time."

"Not at all. The girls are up in their rooms and Stuart is holed up in his office revising his latest novel."

Bianca smiled. She had read a couple of his books and thought he was a great writer who really understood what it took to build characters and a believable plot. She thoroughly enjoyed his work, as did many others.

"So, they've left you all to yourself?"

"Something like that," Madison said. "I was just catching up on a novel I have to review for the magazine. But I needed a break."

"Good, because I just felt like talking to my little sister."

"Call me anytime," she said.

Bianca appreciated the thought, smiling. "Same goes for you."

"Everything all right?" Madison asked curiously.

"Things are great." Bianca paused, realizing she had news to share. "I met someone…"

"That's nice. Tell me more."

"His name is Tanner and he owns a hotel-casino on the Strip."

"Wow!" Madison said. "If you have to meet someone, why not a rich guy?"

"It's not like that," Bianca said defensively.

"I'm just playing with you, sis." Madison laughed. "I realize that in your occupation and town, it's easy to meet someone wealthy, if not easier."

"True," Bianca agreed. At least, in theory.

"So, how did you two meet?"

Bianca explained the car incident, resulting in her bonding with Tanner. "We just seemed to hit it off."

"I'm so happy for you," gushed Madison.

"Thanks." Bianca smiled at her while sipping wine. "We're still a work in progress, but things are good between us right now."

"I'm guessing he's good-looking?"

"Of course," Bianca assured her. *And sexy as hell,* she thought.

"You'll have to send me a picture on your cell phone."

"I will," promised Bianca.

"Can't wait to see him," Madison told her. "So, do you think he could be *the* one?"

Bianca chuckled. "I can't predict the future—been there, done that. But I'm keeping an open mind that we could have a future."

"I'll definitely keep my fingers crossed," Madison told her. "You deserve to be with someone who can make you happy."

"Just as happy as Stuart makes you," Bianca said, recalling how Madison's previous boyfriend broke off their engagement before she went on to meet the right man.

"Exactly," her sister said.

"And from everything you've told me, being a mother to those adorable twins agrees with you, too," Bianca told her.

"I love being a mom," Madison told her. "Carrie and

Dottie keep me grounded and this house full of love and devotion."

"I can see that," Bianca said. "When are you planning to add to your family?" Madison had once mentioned that she and Stuart wanted to have a child one day.

"Soon, hopefully. We're trying, but we're content to enjoy our current little ones till that happens."

"Well, when it does, I'll be happy to be an auntie to another girl or boy," Bianca assured her.

"So will I," Madison tossed back at her.

Bianca chuckled. "Whoa…don't even go there—not yet," she said. "Tanner and I are a long ways from having kids, if we ever do. In fact, we haven't even slept together yet. Much less become a committed couple or talked about marriage."

"I get it," Madison said. "Just putting it out there. Once you and Tanner start to heat things up between the sheets, and assuming it becomes serious, I think you'd make a great mom."

"You do?"

"Yes. You're caring, understanding and patient. You could teach those same qualities to your own children."

Bianca grinned. "I hope you're not giving me too much credit," she cautioned.

"On the contrary, I'm probably not giving you enough credit for what you would bring to the table as a mom. I do know that, as a sister, you've always been there for me when I really needed you."

"I could say the same thing." Bianca realized it was true, even if they had not always recognized it during every stage of their lives.

"Thank you." Madison colored.

"Well, I think I've taken up enough of your reading time," Bianca told her. "I'll let you get back to it."

"Probably should get in a little more before I prepare supper," Madison said. "Keep me posted on what develops between you and Tanner."

"I will." Bianca smiled at her and said goodbye while allowing her mind to wander to just what could develop with Tanner.

On Tuesday, Tanner accompanied Solomon to the Hospital and Community Center for Veterans. Though neither had served in the military, their father had, and it was one way of paying homage to him as well as showing their support for the veterans who lived in Las Vegas.

After spending more than an hour listening to war stories and offering encouragement to wounded veterans, Tanner and Solomon left and drove back to the hotel-casino in Solomon's midnight-blue BMW.

"I've got a meeting scheduled for three o'clock to go over the advertising budget," Solomon said as they walked across the lobby. "Then we need to analyze the data from last week's proceeds."

Tanner smiled. "I'll be there. But if you slip up any on your numbers, I'll show you the door."

Solomon chuckled. "Yeah, right."

"Are you going out tonight with Melanie?"

"Actually, I think it's more like we'll be staying in for the night," Solomon said with a straight face.

"I see." Tanner wondered if his kid brother could actually be getting serious about someone for a change.

"What about you and Bianca?"

"Hadn't made any plans to that effect," Tanner said, "but it would be nice to get together with her tonight."

He thought about the last time he saw her and the kiss that reverberated throughout his body. It took all he had not to take the next step he believed she wanted, too.

"She works for the *Vegas Valley Happenings,* right?" Solomon asked.

"Yeah." Tanner nodded. "So...?"

"So, you could pop by there and surprise her. And while you're at it, you can drum up some publicity for the hotel and casino."

"Good idea," Tanner said. "I just might do that."

Instead, he went to his office and looked up the newspaper on the internet. He found Bianca's name among the staff listings and noticed that she was an entertainment reporter.

He was surprised that they hadn't run into each other before the accident, though perhaps that was a good thing.

*Or had I deprived myself of her beauty and presence by not meeting her sooner?* Tanner wondered. He was just glad they had met and could build upon that.

He asked his secretary, Phyllis, to get the newspaper's publisher and editor, Leslie Ellison, on the phone. They had met before at a function and he thought she was doing a good job running *Vegas Valley Happenings.*

"Hello, Leslie," he said in a friendly tone.

"Hello, Mr. Long," she said. "And congratulations on the opening of Aloha Seas."

"Thank you!"

"How can I help you?"

"Actually, I'm hoping we can help each other," he told her.

"Oh...?"

"I'd like to do a one-on-one interview with the paper."

"Excellent. We'd be happy to send someone over for that," Leslie told him.

"I'd like to do it with Bianca Wagner. I've read some of her pieces and thought they were great."

"Bianca, it is," she agreed. "And she does do a wonderful job with her stories on local entertainment."

"I'm sure she can make me look good and put the spotlight on my new hotel and casino," Tanner said. While he was using this as an excuse to see Bianca again, he also wanted to see this other side of her.

"What time shall we schedule that for?" Leslie asked.

"Tomorrow at three works for me—at my office in the north wing of the hotel, tenth floor, where all the corporate offices are."

"Then she'll see you at three."

"Great. Goodbye."

Tanner sat back in his leather chair, wondering if he should give Bianca a heads-up on the interview. Or see how she reacted to the surprise.

When Bianca stepped into the office, Melanie grabbed her and pulled her aside.

"What?" Bianca asked.

"Look what Solomon gave me." Melanie lifted the diamond heart pendant she was wearing around her neck.

"Nice," Bianca said, admiring it.

"He surprised me with it last night after we made love."

"Guess he must really be into you."

"You think?" Melanie giggled. "We're into each other badly."

Bianca looked at her. "You're in love?"

"Maybe. I'm still trying to process things."

"Do you think he loves you?" wondered Bianca.

"He hasn't said anything yet, but the things he does for me are out of this world."

"I'm happy for you," Bianca told her, while hoping Melanie wasn't misconstruing his actions. As a wealthy man, no doubt used to throwing around money to impress the women he was sleeping with, it certainly didn't mean he was ready to declare his undying love. Much less put a ring on her finger. *But I'm staying out of it,* Bianca thought, wanting to conserve her energy for Tanner and what they might have going on.

She gave Melanie a little hug. "Hope you get everything you want out of this relationship."

"Thanks." Melanie gave a toothy smile. "I feel the same way about you and Tanner. Anyway, better get back to work. I'm late on my deadline, thanks to Solomon preoccupying my mind…and body."

Bianca smiled back and headed to her desk, thinking about her workload, including some events she needed to cover and articles that had to be fine-tuned.

Before she could get there, she was cut off by her boss.

"Got a moment?" Leslie asked.

"Yes." Bianca's eyes focused on the fiftysomething woman.

"I have an assignment for you. I've made arrangements for a one-on-one interview with Tanner Long, the CEO of Aloha Seas, this afternoon."

"Really?" Bianca cocked a brow. Was it coincidence that she was chosen to interview him?

"Yes. Mr. Long specifically asked for you. He's an admirer of your work."

Bianca smiled politely while thinking: *Has he even read anything I've written? Or is this simply part of a seduction scheme?* She wasn't sure if she should be annoyed or flattered.

"No problem," she said. "I'd be happy to interview Tan—Mr. Long."

"Good," Leslie told her. "We might even put him on the front page as the head of one of the Strip's most dynamic hotel-casinos."

Bianca was sure Tanner would love that. Or was that his plan all along? Could he have only been using her to promote the Aloha Seas?

She hated to think along those lines, but knew that there were more than a few sinners in Sin City. She could only hope Tanner wasn't one of them.

# Chapter 7

When Tanner was informed that his appointment had arrived, he glanced at his watch and smiled. *Right on time,* he mused.

He got out of his chair and headed toward the door just as Bianca was entering his office. She looked great as usual, but was not smiling.

"So, what's going on here?" she asked, putting her hand on her hip.

He raised a brow. "Excuse me…?"

Bianca came closer. "Why am I here, Tanner?" she asked insistently.

"Didn't your editor tell you? It's for an interview."

"You've never said anything before about wanting me to interview you. Is that what our romance has been about? You get close to a staff member and then hand-pick her for a *safe* interview?"

"You've got this all wrong." Tanner's brows bridged.

"I never realized you were an entertainment reporter until I saw it on the paper's website yesterday. I just thought it would be nice to see you in your element and open myself up to some questions about the hotel and casino that might interest readers. If I've offended you somehow, I'm sorry. Or if you'd rather keep business and pleasure strictly apart, I can respect that and get someone else to do the interview. It's your choice."

Bianca sucked in a deep breath. "Maybe I'm over-reacting."

"Just a bit," he said wryly.

"But you don't have to rub it in."

He kept a straight face. "I'll try not to."

"I'd be happy to interview you on that note. Thanks for asking, but you could have just called me directly—"

"I wanted to surprise you."

She blinked her eyes. "You did."

"So we're good then?" he asked, to be sure.

She nodded. "We're fine."

Tanner grinned, happy to have defused an awkward situation. He was far more interested in the woman than the reporter. But, in this case, he would refrain from overstepping any boundaries, even if he'd love to kiss her at that moment.

"In that case, why don't we have a seat? You can ask me anything you like about the Aloha Seas."

He led her to a set of plush Queen Anne armchairs surrounding a circular glass table. "Can I get you water, coffee, tea…?"

"Water would be nice."

There was a pitcher of water and some glasses on the table. Tanner filled two glasses, handing her one.

"Thanks," Bianca said, sipping the water. She took a

small digital recorder from her handbag. "Do you mind if I record this?"

"Not at all." He understood that it made it easier for her to quote him directly and just focus on what she wanted to ask him.

"With all the hotels and casinos already on the Strip, what made you decide to add another one?"

Tanner leaned back, but kept his eyes squarely on her. "Well, I've always been of the mind that friendly competition is healthy. I wanted to bring the Hawaiian islands to Vegas in a big way and let the visitors choose which place they'd rather stay and play."

"Hmm…it seems like your vision has gotten off to a strong start," Bianca told him.

"You could say that. Visitors have certainly responded in making Aloha Seas one of the hottest places on the Strip."

"What role did your brother, Solomon Long, who is the chief operating officer, play in bringing this vision to life?" Bianca asked.

"A big one," Tanner told her. "Though it was my brainstorm, this place may have never come to fruition without his talents in helping secure financing and his understanding of what it takes to make the hotel-casino work as a profit maker."

"Sounds like you two are close."

"I'd be less than truthful if I said we are always on the same wavelength," Tanner said. "But, yes, we are pretty close in terms of respect and knowing when and when not to push each other's buttons."

"What is your long-term vision for Aloha Seas?" she asked, eyeing him.

"To make it the best place for entertainment on the Strip, if not all of Las Vegas," Tanner said candidly.

"That's a tall order."

Tanner nodded. "Yes, but it's doable with the solid managerial team we have in place and our commitment to our guests, visitors, investors and the city itself."

"Sounds good," Bianca said, lifting her shoulders.

*"Mahalo!"* Tanner said, happy to use some common Hawaiian words and phrases as part of the Aloha Seas culture.

As he waited for the next question, enjoying singing the praises of Aloha Seas about as much as staring at Bianca's ravishing beauty, the office door burst open. Tanner turned and saw his ex-girlfriend, Angie LeBrock, hastily making her way across the plush carpeting toward them.

Behind her, he saw his secretary, Phyllis, trailing Angie. "I'm sorry, Mr. Long. I told her you were busy but she got past me. Do you want me to call security?"

Tanner got to his feet and responded, "No, I'll handle it."

He watched Phyllis leave and glanced at Bianca, wondering what she must be thinking, before turning his attention to Angie.

"What the hell are you doing here?" he asked, glaring at the attractive and shapely woman with long, chestnut hair.

Her bold green eyes glared at him. "Why didn't you return any of my calls?" she demanded.

"I sent you a text," Tanner said.

"I'm not talking about a damned text!" Angie scowled at him. "You can't just ignore me now that you have gotten what you wanted."

"It's what we both wanted," he insisted.

"So what changed?"

Tanner was tongue-tied. He was embarrassed that

Bianca was sitting there witnessing the entire ordeal. Especially since she was someone he wanted to be with. He felt they may actually have a future together. Or had that now suddenly been jeopardized by Angie's presence?

As though reading his mind, she stood up abruptly. "I think I'd better go…"

"You don't have to," he told her, even though it probably was for the best.

"I believe I do," she retorted. "It's obvious you two have some things to work out. Besides, I think I have enough for the article. I'll show myself out."

Tanner met her eyes guiltily. "I'll call you."

Bianca's lashes fluttered. "Or not…"

She walked away, leaving him alone with Angie.

"Are you sleeping with *her?*" she demanded.

Tanner sighed as he gave her his full attention. "No, not that it's any of your damn business. You and I are through—don't you get that?"

Angie stepped closer. He could smell her pungent perfume.

"That's not what you said when we—"

"I'm saying it now," he broke in. "What we had was fun, but I never promised you anything or asked for anything that you weren't more than willing to give."

"You bastard!" she spat.

"I've been called worse."

Angie licked her lips. "We can have more fun," she said desperately. "Just say when and where."

Tanner sighed. He regretted not being more forthright with her before, but this had to end now. "Listen— what you and I had was a fling. I'm not interested in going there anymore and you shouldn't want to be with someone who doesn't want to be with you. Now do us both a favor and find another rich guy—or even a poor one, I don't care. Just not me. Otherwise, I might start to think that you're stalking me and I'll not only take out a restraining order but will ban you from ever setting foot inside the Aloha Seas. Do we understand each other?"

She shot him a wicked look and then quickly vacated the office.

Much as Bianca had done a few minutes earlier.

*Have I lost her before I even got a chance to progress to the next level?* Tanner asked himself. He called Bianca from his cell phone and it went directly to her voicemail.

What he had to say shouldn't be left in a message, so he headed to the newspaper.


Bianca stepped into the foyer of her house, kicking her shoes off. She was disillusioned about the prospects of a relationship with Tanner after seeing firsthand that his playboy days were not a thing of the past. Certainly not to the pretty young woman he had apparently left hanging and who still wanted him back.

*How can I compete with all the women at his disposal as one of the city's most eligible bachelors?* she wondered. *I need more from a man than good looks, personality and all the money in the world.*

Could she find that with Tanner? Or would she just be another short-term fix for him till the next gorgeous woman came along?

She went into the kitchen, poured herself a glass of wine and took a sip. It helped wash away the bitter taste left in her mouth after leaving Tanner's office.

The doorbell rang. She took another sip of wine and put the glass on the countertop.

When Bianca opened the door, she saw Tanner standing there.

"Can I come in?"

Her first instinct was to say no, but the words didn't seem to want to come out, so she stepped aside.

Tanner walked past her and then turned. "I was told by your boss that you'd left for the day," he said.

"So you came to my house?"

"I needed to see you."

She sighed. "If it's about your girl toy—"

"It's not," he said evenly.

"Then what?" Bianca looked up at his face. "If you're wondering about the article…"

"I'm not here about the article, either."

She met his eyes. "Why are you here?"

Tanner moved up to her, held Bianca's shoulders, and said in a husky voice, "To do this…"

He kissed her passionately, and Bianca knew she could not resist him any longer.

# Chapter 8

Tanner could barely contain himself as he kissed Bianca. A fiery desire overtook them. Their mouths went in circles, attacking each other in a frenzied sequence of hot kisses. His head tilted one way and hers the other as the kiss deepened and their breaths quickened.

He put his hand underneath Bianca's blouse and caressed her nipple. It hardened immediately, and she gave a sigh of satisfaction into his mouth. When he ran his thumb across the other nipple, the reaction was even more to his liking as a moan escaped from Bianca's lips.

Tanner felt his erection trapped inside his pants and begging to be released as their kiss intensified. He ignored it for the moment as his hand slipped under her skirt and made its way between Bianca's legs. He nudged aside her underwear and began to touch her, even while the urge to make love to her continued to build inside him. She was wet and clearly ready for him.

"I want you," he muttered huskily, separating from her mouth and gazing deep into her eyes.

Bianca was trembling. "Do you have protection?" she asked breathily.

"Yes."

"Then take me," she cooed. "Take me right now."

Tanner, realizing her overpowering needs matched his, pulled a foil packet from his pocket and removed the condom. He unzipped his pants and quickly slid the latex over his penis.

Gazing ravenously at Bianca, Tanner slowly backed her against the wall, unable to waste any time removing their clothes. After pushing up her skirt, he moved between Bianca's legs and lifted them before guiding himself into her. He moved deeply inside her, and they began kissing wildly as he thrust himself at Bianca in rapid motions.

Sounds of pleasure escaped their mouths while the urgency of lovemaking brought their bodies together.

It wasn't long before Bianca bit into Tanner's lower lip at the same time she clamped onto his erection, refusing to release him while she climaxed. He winced as his orgasm came, but he continued to move urgently inside her while she moaned with pleasure.

They sucked on each other's mouths and rode the wave of their sexual peak in unison until the sensations slowed and they could catch their breaths. Only then did Tanner release Bianca, allowing her feet to touch the floor.

"Well, that was amazing," Bianca confessed, blushing as she straightened her clothes.

"It was, and that's only the beginning," Tanner told her, his arousal still high.

"You mean there's more?"

"We both needed a quick release," he said. "Now I'd like to make love to you the right way."

"Oh," she said. "So you don't have to leave?"

"Not till we finish what we started."

Bianca smiled. "That sounds good to me."

He grinned eagerly. "Where's your bedroom?"

She took his hand. "Why don't I show you?"

Tanner followed her up a circular staircase, wanting nothing more than to continue the intimacy that could only get better now that they had become sexually acquainted. Clearly Bianca shared this view, giving him more reason for optimism about what was coming next.

Bianca removed her clothes, watching Tanner get turned on with each step. She took pride in her body and was not opposed to a man appreciating it. Especially one with whom she had just had an opening round of satisfying sex and whose own well-developed body was materializing before her very eyes.

He tore open a condom packet. But before he could put it on, Bianca said, "Let me…"

She took it and then gazed with awe at the magnificence of his full erection, excited at the prospect of him pleasuring her. After rolling on the latex, she lifted her chin and found his lips, kissing him passionately while slipping her tongue inside his mouth, tasting and teasing him.

As though that ignited his libido, Tanner scooped Bianca up in his powerful arms and carried her over to the bed, setting her atop a decorative comforter and resting her head on a pillow.

"Lie back and relax," he said softly. "Let me make you feel good."

Bianca already felt good, but was happy to have him

make her feel even better under the weight of his lust-
ful gaze.

Tanner knelt down and began massaging her feet and
toes, the delicate sensations causing Bianca to close her
eyes. He then kissed her feet and ankles.

He worked his way up her legs, applying just the
right amount of pressure with his fingers, masterfully
caressing before kissing and licking the inside of her
thighs.

She felt heat wherever he touched her, making Bianca
utterly aware of his masculinity and sureness.

When Tanner put his face between her legs, she quiv-
ered from the potent sensations of his tongue on her
most private area. It was all she could do not to climax
at that moment, though she suspected this was his wish.

"I want to come with you inside me," she told him.

"Your wish is my command," Tanner said, lifting his
face and regarding her with the type of desire Bianca
had never seen before from a man.

He moved up her body till they were aligned. Then
he opened Bianca's legs wide before propping his hands
on the bed and propelling himself into her like a man
on a mission.

It was a mission Bianca was on, too, as she wrapped
her legs around his buttocks and met his powerful
thrusts halfway each time. Her breasts heaved as they
bounced against his hard chest.

She desperately sought out his mouth, wanting to
feel Tanner's blazing kisses as he made love to her. His
mouth latched on to hers and Bianca gripped his head,
holding him steady while their lips locked succulently.
Their bodies glistened with perspiration as the lovemaking moved into full gear.

Bianca gasped as Tanner hit the mark time and time

again, sending bolts of electricity throughout her body. She felt herself constrict around his erection as it moved deep inside, triggering a powerful climax that caused her to levitate.

"Oh...Tanner," she sang, the pleasure mind-blowing as she clung to him breathlessly.

As though her sounds were the cue to feed his sexual urges, Tanner suddenly turned Bianca over so she was on top of him. Holding her waist, he brought her up and down on his lap.

Sensing the wonderful power she had in that moment, Bianca contracted around him, giving him different degrees of pleasure as she raised and lowered herself on him. She watched his face contort with pleasure when he came with a strong quiver.

She then brought her face down to his, and they kissed heartily while his climax peaked and they relished it together.

When it was over, they continued to kiss in the afterglow before Bianca slid off him and onto the bed.

She sucked in a deep breath. "I guess there really was a lot of gas in the tank after our quickie out there."

Tanner chuckled. "We can ride the rapids anytime you like."

"Anytime?" Bianca suspected that he was just talking fresh after sex, but not necessarily meaning it.

"Sure," he said. "We obviously fit well together in bed. Why deny ourselves whenever the mood strikes?"

"Is that why you carry multiple condoms in your pocket?" she asked curiously. "Just in case you're in the mood to go more than once?"

"No, I wanted to be ready for you. I wanted it to be special and to show you how much I'm into you."

"Good answer," Bianca said, given that she felt the

same way about him. Still, remembering the woman in his office, Bianca couldn't help but say, "Tell me about your ex-girlfriend, or whatever—"

Tanner lifted up, leaning on one elbow. "She was never my girlfriend," he stressed. "We dated for a short time and then it was over."

"Not to her," Bianca said.

"That's because she refused to see what was staring her in the face."

"Which was?" Bianca asked, gazing at him.

"That we were through and nothing could ever change that."

Bianca ignored his hand caressing her skin. "Do you think she finally got the message?"

Tanner paused. "Yeah, I think so."

"You don't sound so sure about that."

"Look, I put my cards on the table, so to speak," he said. "I'd like to believe that she's smart enough to move in another direction—as I have."

"Have you?" Bianca hummed.

Tanner slid his hand along her smooth leg. "Yeah, I have."

She smiled, happy to hear it. "And will there be other ex-girlfriends popping up, trying to get back with you?" she asked.

He grinned. "I doubt it. Most people know when it's time to move on—or when you're good together for the long haul…."

Bianca wondered if what they had would build into something long-term. Or was that a type of commitment Tanner was incapable of making?

## Chapter 9

Tanner sat in the limousine with Solomon. Both were on their cell phones, talking business. Though Tanner listened to what Frank had to say about hotel operations, his mind kept drifting back to Bianca and how incredible they were together. Never before had someone seemed so much his match in bed. That had to be a good sign for the future. But did she feel it, too?

A call came in from *Vegas Valley Happenings* to set up an appointment for a photographer to come to the hotel-casino to shoot some pictures of the place and of Tanner. One of the latter would be used for a front-page photo to accompany Bianca's article.

Tanner was thrilled with the publicity and happier that Bianca was the writer, wanting to do his part to help her along in her career and boost his own at the same time. When he hung up, Tanner saw that Solomon had already completed his phone call, which, from the gist of it, sounded as if he was talking to Melanie, and not necessarily as lovers. Or even friends for that matter.

*Maybe I'm reading too much into that,* Tanner thought. No couple was always on the same page. He wondered if he and Bianca were headed down a rugged path, now that he had smoothed things over regarding Angie. Or was it foolish to even look too far ahead when they were still in the early stages of a relationship?

"You seem a thousand miles away," Solomon commented. "So what's on your mind?"

"I hooked up with Bianca last night," Tanner told him.

"It's about time." Solomon grinned. "How was it?"

"Terrific. Pretty much everything I had imagined, and much more."

Solomon chuckled. "Sounds like she's a keeper."

"Yeah, I don't plan to let her get away anytime soon," Tanner told him.

"I take it she feels the same way?"

"As far as I know."

"So she's cool with who you are and all that?" Solomon asked.

Tanner frowned. "She's not caught up in the rich playboy stuff, if that's what you're asking."

"I'm not, in so many words," he said. "But it is what it is. Not all women can deal with it, even if they say they can."

"Are we talking about Bianca or Melanie?" Tanner asked, looking at him.

"Maybe both."

"Was that Melanie you were talking to on the phone?"

Solomon ran a hand across his mouth. "Yeah, that was her."

"Everything all right between you two?" Tanner asked.

"In bed, yeah. But out of bed, she might be becoming a little too possessive, like some of the other women I've known."

Tanner nodded, thinking of Angie, in particular. "Been there, done that."

"I know," Solomon said.

"So what do you plan to do about it?" Tanner asked, expecting his brother to drop her, as he often did whenever things got a little complicated.

"Nothing at the moment, other than to tell her we can't spend every night—or day, for that matter—together. Hopefully, she'll take it the right way and we'll keep seeing each other."

"That's about all you can do," Tanner said. He didn't get the feeling his brother was in love—which may have been the problem. Then again, maybe Melanie was making Solomon react in a way that suggested there was an emotional attachment between them.

Tanner was already starting to feel an emotional attachment with Bianca. She seemed to be a good fit in his busy and sometimes structured life. That was a good thing, and he always took his gut instincts seriously. Currently, his gut was telling him that there was no limit to how far they could take their relationship. Meanwhile, he looked forward to their next meeting and what might happen as a result.

On Saturday, Bianca was up early. She went for her usual run and spent much of it thinking about Tanner and the hours they had spent together the other night. The man certainly knew how to please a woman in bed, leaving her wanting more. And it worked like a charm—she couldn't get their lovemaking out of her mind.

*I'll have to try,* she told herself, getting back to the house. *At least for a little while,* since she had other things on her agenda for the day. There would be plenty of time later to recall every detail of their intimacy and think about what they could do the next time to further their mutual satisfaction.

Bianca took a shower. Forty-five minutes later, she had dressed and was on her way to Hope Ranch, the safe house for teenage runaways and ex-prostitutes operated by her friend Vicky Poole.

*I can think of so many people to blame for these poor girls,* thought Bianca. But what good would that do? The important thing was that they now had a chance to make things right before it was too late to try to make something of their lives.

Though she played only a small part in that, Bianca took it seriously. It was a good way to give back something to those who were less fortunate than she was, often through no fault of their own.

"Hey," Vicky said, greeting her at the door of the house on the ten-acre ranch outside the city limits.

Bianca smiled. "Hi! My virtual sleeves are rolled up and I'm ready to go to work."

Vicky grinned. "That's what I like to hear. And the girls will like it, too. You always bring something positive to the table that they can all take away from."

Bianca fed off that energy as she spoke to the teens, any of whom could have been her kid sister. She told them about her life, asked about theirs and participated in the chores that were required for everyone who stayed at the ranch. After that, they played touch football for a while. As she watched the girls giggling and having fun, it seemed to Bianca that they were finally getting to enjoy some semblance of the childhood that had been so cruelly taken away from them.

Later, Bianca and Vicky took a walk through the grounds.

"You're doing great things here," Bianca pointed out. "I can see changes in the girls each time I come."

Vicky smiled. "Thanks. They all deserve a lot more than they've gotten out of life so far."

"So do you," Bianca said, noting that her love life had been up and down, as well. "Are you still with—"

"Derrick?" Vicky finished. "No, he moved on and so have I. My new guy's name is Jefferson. He teaches at UNLV where I'm taking some classes. We've only gone out on a few dates, but everything's been great so far."

"That's awesome!" Bianca said and gave her a high five. "Hope it works out."

"Speaking of working out—what about you and Tanner Long?" Vicky asked.

Bianca smiled. "We're seeing each other now."

"Oh, really?" Vicky pretended to be hurt. "And you're just telling me this now?"

Bianca laughed. "I was going to get to it. Like you and Jefferson, we're just getting started in our relationship."

"So there is more to the man than good looks, money and hotel-casinos," Vicky said.

Bianca eyed her thoughtfully. "Yes, quite a bit more."

"Do tell."

"Well, he's smart, athletic, well-traveled, generous, charitable—"

"And good in bed?" Vicky asked wickedly.

Bianca grinned. "Yes, that too."

Vicky chuckled. "So in other words, he's the complete package?"

"Yes, I'd say so," Bianca had to admit.

"What about the playboy, most-eligible-bachelor tag?"

Bianca looked at her thoughtfully. "It's part of who he was in the past, but it doesn't mean that's all he wants out of life."

"My sentiments exactly," Vicky said, smiling. "You've given him something to think about in turning his life and love in a whole new direction."

"No one said anything about love," cautioned Bianca. She was certainly open to developing such feelings both ways, but it was too early to go there just yet.

"True, but that's always an option when two people are in sync."

"We'll see," Bianca said. "Right now, I just want to date the man and see where his head is as we go along."

"I'm singing the same tune with Jefferson," stated Vicky. "If it's meant to go all the way to the altar, it will."

Bianca smiled at the notion, wishing only the best for her friend. And for herself, as well. Would Tanner ever be the marrying type? Would she?

She chose to put those thoughts on hold and focus on the present as they worked on their relationship—without any pressures one way or the other.


Tanner was at home sitting at his patio when he called Bianca. He had been thinking about her and how good they were together.

When she accepted the video chat, he watched as her face appeared on his iPad screen. "Hello, gorgeous."

"Hello back, handsome." She flashed her pretty teeth.

"If you're not busy tonight, I'd like to invite you to see Kendre Kelly perform in our concert hall."

"I love Kendre Kelly!" Bianca declared. "And I'd love to go to the concert with you."

Tanner smiled broadly. "Great. She signed with us to do a gig for six months. She's gotten rave reviews. I've been meaning to catch her act and finally found time tonight."

"It should be fun."

"It will be, with you there," he assured her.

"Oh, Tanner." Her face lit. "Keep that up and I might start to get used to it."

"That's the plan," Tanner said with a chuckle, but he was quite serious. He felt good and happy when he was around her and saw no reason not to milk it for all it was worth.

"Well, I certainly wouldn't want to ruin your plans," Bianca said.

"I'm glad you said that, because after the show I thought we'd come up to my place for a nightcap."

"Just a nightcap?" she teased him.

"Maybe for starters…"

"Hmm…so there's more, then?"

He laughed, getting turned on by her implication. "Yes, there's more, but you'll have to wait and see to find out."

"I'm sure I could use my imagination to hazard a guess," Bianca told him, chuckling.

"It couldn't possibly measure up to the real thing," Tanner insisted provocatively.

"Oh, really…?"

"Not in this lifetime," he promised.

"In that case, I look forward to your plans for the evening after the concert."

His eyes crinkled as he smiled at her. "So do I."

After he hung up, Tanner made a few business calls and then got ready for the evening.

Bianca tried on three different outfits before settling on a red sleeveless satin sheath and slipping into matching platform pumps. It wasn't as though she needed to impress Tanner with her sense of style or compete with celebrities such as the talented Kendre Kelly.

Or did she?

*I'd like him to keep noticing me, whether we're at a concert or not,* Bianca thought, pulling her hair back into a loose bun. It was called being a woman, and men simply appreciated well-dressed women.

Never mind the fact that their clothes were likely to come off when they got to his place, if she'd read him correctly. Though she was certain she had, since she wanted his body as much as he wanted hers and couldn't wait to make love to him again.

She dabbed on a touch of perfume, sure it would appeal to Tanner's sense of smell.

When the doorbell rang, she opened it to find Tanner standing there with a nice grin on his face and a huge bouquet of colorful roses.

"You look beautiful tonight," he said coolly and handed her the flowers.

"Thank you," she gushed, accepting the gorgeous array and quickly placing them on the hallway table behind her without taking her eyes off Tanner. She admired his white sport coat, navy blue slacks and yellow shirt. "And you look very handsome."

"Thanks." He grinned. "Just trying to keep up."

"I don't think you need to try very hard, Mr. Most Eligible…"

Tanner met her eyes. "I'm no longer eligible or available with you in my life."

Bianca smiled at his words, wanting to believe he meant them. "That's good to know."

"You're pretty good to know, too," he said smoothly.

"So are you," she said.

"Well, I'm glad we agree on that."

Her lashes fluttered. "Did you think we wouldn't?"

"Not for one second." He regarded her seductively. "We'd better get out of here before I say 'forget about the damned concert, and let's just make our own music.'"

Bianca was certainly tempted to have him all to herself for the night, to do as she pleased and allow him to do the same. But if she wanted to be seen with him, if he truly was her man, this was a great place to start.

"You're right," she told him. "Besides, there will be time for that later." She was counting on it.

"You can bet on that without losing a cent!" Tanner assured her.


The concert was everything Bianca expected and more. Kendre Kelly was a great jazz vocalist who knew how to work the audience. Bianca had several of Kendre's albums but felt she was even better live. Tanner seemed to be in agreement, nodding in appreciation of each song. He had his arm around Bianca, making her feel as though she was his special lady.

When the concert was over, Tanner introduced her to Kendre, who was more petite than Bianca realized, but every bit as attractive with mounds of sable hair surrounding a heart-shaped face.

"I'm a big fan of yours," Bianca told her sincerely in the dressing room.

Kendre brushed aside her hair. "That's so sweet of you to say."

"Count me on your fan list, too," Tanner told her.

"Thanks. I really appreciate the opportunity to perform here, Tanner. Singing in Vegas is like nowhere else on earth."

He smiled. "I agree with you there, and it's me who appreciates your taking time from your schedule to spend a few months at the Aloha Seas."

"It's a win-win," she declared.

"Yeah, I believe it is," he said.

Kendre licked her glossy lips and regarded Bianca. "By the way, you guys look great together."

*"Mahalo!"* Bianca told her in keeping with the hotel's Hawaiian theme.

Tanner held Bianca's hand. "Yeah, *mahalo*."

"I just hope I'm as lucky and find someone who can put up with my demanding schedule," Kendre said enviously.

"I'm sure you will," Tanner told her.

From what Bianca had heard, Kendre had no shortage of lovers moving in and out of her life. Obviously, though, Mr. Right had not come along for her yet. Maybe he would, now that she was going to be in Vegas performing for a few months. Bianca was pretty sure that Kendre would have countless potential suitors lining up.

## Chapter 10

"This is it," Tanner told her the moment they got off the private elevator and stepped inside the penthouse suite.

"Wow!" Bianca couldn't help but say as she took a sweeping glance around the suite with its bamboo flooring, elegant furnishings and amazing views from floor-to-ceiling windows on all sides.

"You like?" Tanner held her waist, peering into her eyes.

"I love," she responded succinctly. "It's beautiful!"

"I agree, but not half as beautiful as you are."

Bianca tingled inside, still trying to get used to the type of attention and praise he was giving her. "You make me feel that way," she admitted.

"I try." He tilted his head perfectly and kissed her lips.

She loved the taste of his kiss and, in that setting,

could have continued to kiss him all night. But she was sure he wanted to do more than that, as did she.

Bianca unlocked their lips. "What about that nightcap you promised me?"

"That can wait," he said hungrily. "I'd much rather introduce you to the bedroom."

She gazed eagerly into his eyes and said, "So introduce me to it."

He took her hand and led her down a hall with twists and turns until they reached the master suite. Like the rest of the place, it was perfect, with stylish black furnishings and a king-size brass bed that Bianca had no trouble imagining herself in—with him.

"So, what do you think?" Tanner asked her with amusement.

"I think we need to see how well we fit together in that bed of yours," she told him shamelessly.

He grinned. "Something tells me the fit will be incredible."

"Something tells me that you're right."

Boldly, Bianca began removing his clothes until he was stark naked. Then she pushed him onto the bed and made him watch while she let her hair down before slowly and sensuously taking off her dress, bra and panties, leaving on her pumps as something she believed might turn him on.

She found some condoms in the nightstand drawer and removed one. But before she put it on him, she wanted to pleasure him orally. She climbed on the bed, lowered her face to his erection and took him her mouth, bringing him to the back of her throat.

She wrapped her tongue around the tip and licked, feeling his body trembling from the exquisite pleasure.

"You're killing me," groaned Tanner, his eyes shut tight.

Turned on by having him helpless to her seduction, Bianca moved her mouth up and down the length of him several times, deliberately teasing him to the brink before laying off, so as to stretch the time out as long as possible.

Even while stimulating him, she became aware of Tanner contorting his upper body so that his face met the place between her legs. "Two can play that game," he declared triumphantly.

Before she could react to his mouth kissing her clitoris, they were hotly engaged in a delicious sixty-nine.

It was all Bianca could do not to come the moment Tanner's tongue ran across her tender spot. But she fought back the joyous urge, concentrating on continuing to appease him.

Soon they had both climaxed from the oral gratification, holding each other's quivering bodies in place while the sensations ran their course.

Still reeling from the mutual orgasm, Tanner was ready for a second round, and clearly Bianca was, too, as she placed the condom on him. She climbed on top, arched her back and slid onto his erection until he was deep inside her, whereupon she began galloping like a prize-winning mare.

Tanner lusted for her as never before as Bianca moved up and down him. She put her breasts in his face, allowing him to suck her nipples. He held her buttocks firmly and brought his body up to meet hers every time. The urge to climax was maddening, but he exerted willpower to hold off, wanting them to achieve the ultimate satisfaction together.

When Bianca began sucking his lips and moaning harmonically, Tanner felt her body quiver as she contracted around his phallus. While his libido threatened to boil over, he seized the moment, turning them over so they were in the missionary position.

As Bianca raised her legs off the bed, Tanner propelled his throbbing manhood into her in a rapid succession of strokes, hitting the mark every time and loving the feel of their passion making his blood run red-hot.

"Don't stop," purred Bianca, clawing at his back, strangled sounds of pleasure coming from her mouth.

"I couldn't even if I tried," Tanner groaned lasciviously, draping her legs across his powerful arms and inserting himself into her in fluid, even strokes. As his orgasm swept through him, he sought Bianca's mouth, and they kissed passionately with their tongues as their dampened bodies came together in blazing sexual satisfaction.

Even as the intense sensations began to wane, they continued going at it, enjoying the pleasures of their intimacy as though unable to pull apart.

When they were finally finished, Tanner got off Bianca and fell onto the bed. He sucked in a deep breath and said, "What a way to welcome you to my home!"

"I'll say," she told him with a chuckle. "Is that your standard greeting?"

"Definitely not," he assured her. "There's nothing typical about being with you like this."

"Are you sure about that?"

"Yeah." He kissed her smooth shoulder. "Positive."

"In that case, I'm certainly glad you invited me to your palace."

Tanner grinned. "For a queen like you, anytime."

"I'll remember that," Bianca promised.

"I'm counting on it," he said.

"Now, what about that nightcap?" she tossed at him teasingly.

He met her eyes playfully. "I thought we just had it."

"Is that what you call what we just did?"

"Actually, I could think of another name or two."

She chuckled. "I'm sure you could."

Tanner put his hand on the moist valley between her breasts. "Now, regarding that nightcap…"

"Yes?" Bianca watched his eyes.

"Why don't we start with this and go from there.…"

He leaned over and gave her a deep, openmouthed kiss. As she wrapped her arms around his head, pinning their lips together, Tanner felt his erection return and knew they might have to delay that drink again.

When Bianca woke up, she reached for Tanner, wanting to feel his hard body next to hers. But his side of the bed was empty. She glanced at the clock and saw that it was nearly nine in the morning.

She hadn't meant to sleep that long, even if this was her off day. But having torrid sex all night could do that to you, especially with a lover as thorough as Tanner.

*I hope I'm not making a mistake getting too comfortable with him,* Bianca thought. *I don't want to throw all my emotions and carnal desires into something that won't last.*

On the other hand, she was all about taking chances in a relationship. This was, after all, Las Vegas, where everyone gambled on something. Including a shot at love.

Though that subject may have been premature, Bianca couldn't help but keep it in the back of her mind as a possibility, considering the person she had become attached to.

Speaking of whom, where was he, anyway? Had he gone back to running his hotel-casino, leaving her alone to show herself out?

Rolling out of bed, Bianca slipped on one of Tanner's shirts and went in search of him.

She found him standing over a granite countertop in a gourmet kitchen that seemed to have everything a cook could want.

"Well, good morning, sleepyhead," Tanner said cheerfully.

"Good morning." She strode barefoot toward him. "Why didn't you wake me?"

"Because I figured you needed your beauty rest after last night."

"I did," she admitted, suppressing a yawn. "So did you."

"I can usually get by on only a few hours of sleep," he told her. "Besides, I wanted to make you breakfast in bed. Hope you like waffles."

"I love them." Bianca smiled, and her taste buds ignited. "But don't you have to go to work?"

"That's the beauty of being CEO, I delegate tasks to others," Tanner said. "I also do a lot of my work from home, thanks to my cell phone and iPad."

"I see." She cozied up to him. "Hope you don't mind that I borrowed your shirt."

Tanner regarded her lasciviously. "Not at all. It looks very sexy on you."

"You would say that."

"Because it's true." He grinned. "But then again, anything would look sexy on you."

She flashed her eyes at him doubtfully. "You think so?"

"I *know* so." He kissed her tenderly on the lips.

"Nice," Bianca said, tasting the kiss.

"This may be even nicer...." Tanner sliced off a piece of waffle, dipping it into a pitcher of maple syrup. "Here, taste that and tell me what you think."

She tasted it as syrup dribbled down her chin. "It's delicious!"

"Here, let me wipe that off," he said, and licked the syrup from her chin. "Is that better?"

"Yes," she mumbled, becoming aroused with his sexual way of solving many problems.

"Good. Now have a seat and let me serve you breakfast."

Bianca was only too happy to accommodate his request. Especially since she planned to return the favor one day when he stayed over at her house. Or was she thinking too far ahead, even if this relationship did seem to be moving into high gear?

# Chapter 11

"Where did you learn to cook like this?" Bianca asked curiously as she ate a piece of waffle while eyeing the hash browns on her plate.

"My mother was a great cook, and my father, too," Tanner told her. "They passed it down to their sons, though only one of them took it to heart."

"Lucky you and those who get to taste your cooking."

"Thanks," he said. "I guess I just enjoy using my hands to do good things."

Bianca chuckled. "Umm, yes, you certainly do have a way with those hands of yours that can do some very good things."

He laughed. "Naughty girl."

She laughed, too. "Sorry, couldn't resist."

"It's cool—because I'm finding it harder and harder to resist you."

Bianca showed her teeth. "Is that right?"

"Yeah, it's true," Tanner said, and scooped up some hash browns.

"Well, you're pretty irresistible yourself," she told him honestly.

"Guess we truly are on the same wavelength as to where we are in this relationship."

She wiped syrup from her lips with a napkin and gazed at him. "So, we are in a relationship?"

"Yes, I'd say so," he said. "Wouldn't you?"

"I would," she admitted happily. "I just wasn't sure how you defined it, given your track record as a Vegas playboy."

Tanner grinned. "The playboy label aside, I'm not afraid to be in a real relationship with an attractive, smart and sexy lady."

"That's good to know." Bianca smiled at him. "And I'm not afraid to be involved with a handsome, successful businessman."

"That's even better to know." He leaned forward. "So we'll just have to put up with each other and leave everyone else to envy."

"Sounds like a plan to me." In Bianca's mind, everything he had said was something she was more than amenable to. This surprised her somewhat, as she was normally more on guard with someone who seemed to have it all, including his choice of stunning women. But he had chosen her, causing Bianca to let down her guard and slowly but surely begin to surrender her heart.

"What do you say we go for a dip in the pool?" Tanner suggested.

"I'd love to, but I didn't bring my suit," Bianca responded.

"That's not a problem."

"You'd rather I swam naked?" she asked jokingly.

Tanner laughed. "Now that's a thought for when I get my own private pool. Actually, I have a swimsuit for you—or a few...."

Bianca drew her head back with a frown. "You keep swimsuits around for your girlfriends to pass from one to the next?"

"Not quite," he said. "While you were sleeping, I had one of my employees from our Aloha Water Wear store bring up several swimsuits that I thought were your size for you to pick and choose from."

"Where are they?" she asked with excitement.

"In the living room. They are laid out and waiting for you."

She chuckled, amazed at his style. "Is there anything you don't think of?"

He grinned. "Not much, especially if it fits into my plans."

Bianca wiped her mouth again and rose. "Well, I guess I'd better go see what you've got for me."

She went into the living room and saw the swimsuits on display. Holding them up to her, all seemed to fit and were nice to look at. Of course, she knew that Tanner was most interested in them looking nice on her.

"Do you prefer the one-piece or bikini?" she asked him.

He grinned. "Whatever you like," he said diplomatically. "I want you to feel comfortable wearing it."

"Good answer." She smiled and grabbed a purple bikini top along with a sexy matching ruffled bottom. Though it left little to the imagination, she was proud of her body and wasn't afraid to show some skin. Certainly not to someone who had already seen her from head to toe. "I choose this one."

"Excellent choice," Tanner declared with satisfaction.

"And what about you? Do I get to choose what you wear?" Bianca teased him.

"If you want, but I'm afraid there are only two choices. I'll be happy to go with whichever one you like."

Bianca accepted that, though doubting that he would care one way or the other. To her, it was just a means of showing equality and having fun in their relationship, things she considered important for any relationship to work.

They did a few laps in the pool, which was bordered by sand, as though they were swimming at a Hawaiian resort or in the Pacific Ocean. Bianca had fun testing her limits and trying to keep up with Tanner. Or waiting for him to catch up to her.

They laughed, splashed and kicked like little kids. Then touched, teased and kissed liked adults.

"You're really good at this," Tanner told her, barely out of breath.

"Did you think I wouldn't be?" she asked daringly.

"Something tells me I'd be a fool to ever underestimate any of your capabilities."

"I have a feeling the same might be true for me, where you're concerned."

He smiled and gave her a quick kiss before saying, "Race you back across."

Tanner took off and Bianca went after him. She caught up easily enough, suspecting he had let her, but not complaining one bit.

They went back up to his room, showered and made love again, giving Bianca more reason for relishing the bond they had established on so many levels. She only hoped that she never woke up to find it was nothing but a good dream.

* * *

The next week, Bianca was at work when Melanie came up to her desk. She had a down look on her face.

"What's wrong?" Bianca asked.

"Nothing."

"You know something's wrong and you know you want to tell me—so spill it."

Melanie rolled her eyes. "Solomon and I had a fight."

Bianca flashed her a surprised look. Melanie had been all smiles recently when showing off the diamond heart pendant Solomon had given her as a gift. Though she wasn't wearing it at the moment.

"About what?"

Melanie shrugged. "Same old stuff most people fight about...time apart, time together, money, sex—"

"So are you spending too much time together or apart?" Bianca wondered.

"Both, I think."

"What's up with the money issue?"

Melanie shrugged. "He has too much, I have too little. Sometimes I feel like he uses it to his advantage to put me down."

"I thought things were going great between you two," Bianca said.

"They are, I guess. At least, most of the time," Melanie said.

"Problems in the bedroom, too?"

Melanie shook her head. "No, he's great in bed. It's just sometimes he doesn't seem to be there. It's like he's with me and someone else at the same time."

Bianca's eyes widened. "You think he's cheating on you?"

"I don't know. He says he isn't."

"Maybe you should take him at his word," Bianca suggested. "Don't go looking for trouble."

"I'm not," Melanie insisted. "I just want to have an honest relationship for a change, where we see eye to eye on the things that count."

"Yeah, don't we all." Bianca looked at her desk thoughtfully. That certainly had not been the case for every relationship she had been in. Often, it was quite the contrary. But she considered it a learning experience and a part of life that everyone had to go through.

"How are things with you and Tanner?" Melanie asked.

Bianca smiled, "Great. He's been all that and then some."

"That's really nice. I hope it lasts."

*I hope so, too,* Bianca thought, feeling optimistic that her knight in shining armor was as much into her as she was into him. "We're taking things one day at a time," she told Melanie.

"So are we," Melanie said tonelessly. "Even if sometimes the days and nights seem like they're going nowhere fast."

"Just don't put too much pressure on him or yourself," Bianca warned. "Otherwise you'll only end up second-guessing everything." Having said that, she suddenly realized she would do well to take her own advice.

A few days later, Bianca had been having lunch with Tanner at the Aloha Seas until he had to leave with his general manager, Frank, to deal with an issue at a gaming table. Though Tanner promised to come back, she let him off the hook, needing to head out herself for an interview with someone at another hotel-casino on the

Strip. But she promised to call Tanner later to see if they could get together.

He left her with a kiss that had her lips still tingling when she left the restaurant.

She hadn't expected to run into Solomon minus Melanie. Bianca considered their recent conversation about Solomon.

"Hey," he said coolly.

"Hey," she told him.

"I was hoping to catch you before you left."

Bianca lifted a brow, curious. "What's up?"

"I'm planning a birthday party for Tanner this Saturday," Solomon said.

"I didn't know his birthday was coming up," she said, realizing that they hadn't gone that far in learning each other's life stories.

"Well, he usually tries to downplay it as no big deal." Solomon twisted his mouth. "Me, I like to make it a big deal, just as I do my own birthday. Anyway, it's going to be a surprise party."

"That sounds like fun." Bianca regarded him. "So, how can I help?"

"Actually, that's what I wanted to talk to you about. Since Tanner is always hanging around and is very observant, it's hard to put one over on him." Solomon met her eyes. "I was hoping you could distract him—keep him away from the Aloha Seas until about three o'clock."

"Hmm...I can certainly try," she said. "But Tanner has a mind of his own and will probably figure out that something's up."

"Or not," Solomon said flatly. "He really cares about you, and I'm sure if you put your mind to it you can keep him busy. Frank and I will handle things on this end, as far as what's going on and what isn't—if you know what I mean."

Bianca wasn't quite sure what his thoughts were in terms of keeping Tanner busy, and perhaps it was best that she didn't use her imagination. But she was sure that, at the end of the day, Solomon just wanted to show his brother a good time. Since she felt the same way about her sister, this made sense to her.

"I'll keep Tanner away until three," she promised.

"Thanks." Solomon grinned. "The party will be held in the Kaanapali Ballroom."

"I'm sure it'll be a lot of fun."

"Yeah, for real."

Bianca smiled. "So, how are things with you and Melanie?" she asked casually.

"Okay." Solomon gazed at her. "Why, did she say something?"

"No, not really." Bianca certainly didn't want to get in the middle of their relationship, though she felt obligated to look out for her friend since she felt responsible for the two of them getting together. "Well, she said you guys had a fight."

"I wouldn't call it that," Solomon said. "We just had a little disagreement. Everything's cool now."

Bianca smiled. "That's good to know."

"Yeah." He grinned crookedly. "Well, I have to run. If Tanner gets suspicious that something's up—"

"He won't," she assured him confidently. "Not if I can help it."

"Cool. Later."

Bianca watched him walk away. Now she had to think of a clever way to keep Tanner preoccupied without tipping her hand.

# Chapter 12

Tanner met with his attorney and good friend, Chuck, at his office to discuss business.

Afterward, Chuck poured them both a glass of scotch. "How did things go with the lady you went out on a date with the last time we met?" he asked. "Or have several other good-looking women passed through by now?"

Tanner laughed and sipped his drink. "Actually, we're seeing each other."

"Bravo, buddy!" Chuck declared. "She must really be putting the hex on you, if you're actually dating and admitting to it."

"Well, I don't think she's into black magic," Tanner told him humorously. "But Bianca does have some sort of hold on me."

"I can see that."

"We just seem to get along well, and the pieces fit."

"Like a puzzle?" asked Chuck.

"More like a man and woman," Tanner responded truthfully.

"I'll go along with that. So, when do I get to meet this lady that's got you wrapped around her finger?"

"Why don't we get together next week," Tanner suggested, while thinking about the ways he and Bianca had wrapped their hands and limbs around each other. "You can bring Deloris and we can have dinner somewhere."

"Sounds good to me," Chuck said, sipping his scotch. "I know Deloris will be all for it, too. She's definitely up for meeting someone new and not as boring as some of the women she hangs out with these days."

Tanner grinned. "Bianca's anything but boring, so I think she and Deloris will get along just fine."

"Then it's a date. Just text me with the details and we'll be there."

"Will do."

"What about Solomon?" asked Chuck.

Tanner sat back. "What about him?"

"Has he also renounced his playboy ways and found someone to hang with more long-term?"

Tanner thought about it. "Yeah, he's seeing someone. I don't know how serious it is, though."

"Well, maybe he'll surprise us," Chuck said.

"Maybe he will."

"In the meantime, if you play your cards right, you just might have hit the jackpot with Bianca."

Tanner laughed, amused by the gambling analogy. "You never know." Even he didn't know at this point if what they had was the jackpot. Or if there were still more cards that should be dealt in their relationship before they would see precisely where it was headed.

* * *

Bianca had Tanner spend the night as part of her plan to keep him away from the hotel-casino until three the following afternoon. She suspected that they would have no problem staying in bed and making love all day, as he was insatiable. The feeling was mutual, as he brought out desires in her as no other ever had.

But she decided to do something fun outside to keep Tanner's attention. If there was still time, they could always head back to her place for some passion.

"What's this?" Tanner asked, entering the kitchen after taking a shower.

Bianca smiled at him. "Just a little something I put together. I thought we'd go on a picnic," she told him evenly.

"A picnic?"

"Yes, it's where two people feed each other some snacks from a basket and otherwise enjoy each other's company," she teased him, while wondering if he would confess that it was his birthday.

"I know what a picnic is," he said, chuckling. "And where will this picnic take place?"

"Desert Breeze Park seems like a perfect spot," Bianca said as she put some grapes into the basket. "And it's also a romantic way to spend the afternoon, don't you think?"

*Say yes,* she thought.

Tanner walked up to her and slipped his hands around Bianca's waist. The scent of his pleasant after-shave crossed her nostrils. "Sounds romantic, but—"

"No buts," Bianca said, putting a finger to his lips as she sensed he wanted to go to work. "I'm sure they won't miss you if you come in a little late. I wouldn't want to see this nice picnic basket go to waste."

She gazed pleadingly into his eyes, and his gleamed back at her.

"I wouldn't want that, either," he told her. "Picnic it is."

"Thank you." Bianca kissed him on the mouth, lingering longer than she had planned to, but the man was irresistible.

Tanner licked his lips. "You can thank me later."

She flashed him a lascivious look. "Oh, I intend to."

*Dodged that bullet,* she thought. Now it was up to Solomon to take care of the rest.

Tanner phoned Frank en route to the park, informing him that he wouldn't be coming in just yet. Frank told him they had everything under control.

Solomon pretty much said the same thing, while suggesting he might take off early himself for a little bedroom frolic. Tanner took that to mean things were back on track with him and Melanie. Not that he wanted to micromanage his brother's love life any more than he wanted Solomon to manage his.

It was just that he didn't want anything to derail his romance with Bianca simply because things fell apart with his brother and her girlfriend. Tanner hoped it never came to that.

He gazed at Bianca's attractive profile as she drove. Since it was her plan to spend the day together, he never considered having Johan drive them in the limousine. It was her show, and he was happy to allow her to run it. Besides, Tanner thought it was sexy to watch Bianca behind the wheel.

Though not quite as sexy as seeing her naked and giving him her body to please and caress to his heart's content.

Tanner's birthday crossed his mind. He'd never been big on celebrating turning a year older. He was only a few years from forty and wanted to start thinking about settling down and having a family. Bianca seemed like the type of lady he could build such a family with. Or was that even something that interested her? The last thing he needed was to freak her out about having children and getting married, though not necessarily in that order.

*I'll have to take my chances sooner rather than later and see where her head is on this score,* he thought.

Bianca turned to him and smiled. "You look nice in my car."

Tanner grinned. "So do you."

"We'll have to do this more often," she said.

"Anytime."

"You can even drive sometimes, if you want." She glanced his way. "You do drive, don't you?"

He laughed. "Yeah, I do. Sometimes I borrow Solomon's BMW when I want to hit the road and be alone. I've even been known to occasionally take the limo out for a spin."

Bianca giggled. "Now *that* I'd have to see."

"You will one of these days," he promised.

She turned onto Spring Mountain Road and a few minutes later pulled into Desert Breeze Park. "We're here."

Tanner grinned. "Can't wait to see what you packed for the picnic."

"Hope you're hungry," she warned.

"Starving," he told her, mainly to make her happy

after she'd put forth the effort to do something romantic as a couple, aside from spending time in bed.

Bianca fed Tanner some grapes and watched as his lips moved sexily while he chewed.

"Your turn," he told her, grabbing a grape and placing it in her mouth.

She felt embarrassed as a little grape juice spilled down her chin.

Tanner chuckled. "Let me wipe that for you." He lifted a paper napkin and dabbed her mouth and chin. "There, that's better."

"I may need you around often to take care of such problems," she teased him.

"I like being around you, and more is better," he said, holding her gaze.

"I agree," Bianca said, wondering where on earth he had been all her life. But the important thing was that he was here now. She watched as he opened a bottle of white wine and half-filled two goblets, passing her one.

Tanner grinned. "Can't get much better than this. Sunshine, wine and you. Tasty all the way around."

Bianca grinned. "Hmm," she said happily, sipping the wine as they sat at the picnic table. She passed him a chicken sandwich and he dug right in to it.

"Delicious." Tanner swallowed and took another bite. "You know, I really could get used to this type of thing."

"So could I." She bit into her sandwich while wondering just how far things could actually go between them. Or was it wise to wonder too much?

"Have you ever thought about having a family?" Tanner asked casually.

Bianca looked at him. "Doesn't everyone?"

"Not everyone wants a family, for one reason or another," he pointed out.

"That's true." She drank her wine thoughtfully. "Yes, I'd like to have a family someday. How about you?"

"Yeah, me too. Solomon and I have talked about it every now and then. Since we're the last of our bloodline, we'd both like to have kids to carry on the family name."

Her eyes widened. "Is that the only reason?"

"It would be an extension of my commitment to the mother—and vice versa."

Bianca liked hearing that, even if the word *love* was not mentioned. Though it hardly went without saying, he'd implied as much. "I'm sure you'd make a great dad."

"I know I would," Tanner said confidently. "And you'd make a great mom."

"I hope so." In truth, she wasn't sure if she would measure up to being a good mother. Not like her sister, who had proven to be a natural mom.

"You certainly would know how to nourish your offspring, if feeding the guy in your life is any indication," Tanner told her, smiling.

"In that case, I guess you're good practice," Bianca said.

"Practice makes perfect," he declared.

She fluttered her lashes. "Is that what you are—perfect?"

"I'm not, but I think you are."

"Hmm…" Bianca wasn't too comfortable being put on a pedestal. Yet he somehow made her seem worthy of it. "Well, I could say the same thing about you."

"Maybe it's better if you show me," he challenged.

She gladly accepted the challenge, taking hold of

his cheeks and pressing her mouth into his for a long, passionate kiss.

"Does that show you?" Bianca asked, after pulling away.

Tanner beamed. "Yeah, it's a start."

"A start, huh?" She glanced at her watch and saw that it was two-thirty. By the time they got to the hotel-casino, it would be the top of the hour for his birthday surprise. "What more can a girl do?"

He grinned intimately. "I'm sure we'll be able to think of something...."

"I'm sure we will." Bianca felt the need to be with him sexually, but would have to put that on hold for now. "I think I've kept you from work long enough. I'll drive you there and hang out at your place until you get off."

"Okay, but I intend to do as little work as possible today, so I can get up there to keep you company."

"It's a deal," Bianca said, and stuck out her hand for a friendly handshake.

Tanner took her hand, kissing it and sending streaks of desire shooting up her arm and throughout her body. She bit her lip and imagined what she would give him for his birthday, apart from the surprise party.

## Chapter 13

When Tanner passed through the casino with Bianca, he mainly just wanted to show off to her what he hadn't previously. They strolled past slot machines and the general gambling area, where both serious and recreational gamblers coexisted peacefully. But she seemed distracted and was ready to go back to the hotel. He assumed that she wanted to go up to his suite at that moment to make love, though she had indicated otherwise.

"What's in there?" Bianca asked him, after they had taken a short cut and were standing outside the Kaanapali Ballroom.

"That's where we have important functions for those who can afford to pay for them," he told her.

She met his eyes. "Can I take a look?"

"Of course."

"I'm just curious," she said. "Maybe the newspaper will want to have their annual Christmas party here this year."

"You're more than welcome to," Tanner said as he opened the double doors to the room.

A large gathering in the room shouted together, "Happy Birthday, Tanner!"

Tanner was speechless.

Solomon walked up to them, grinning broadly. "Good job, Bianca. I couldn't have pulled this off without you."

Tanner eyed Bianca with surprise. "You knew about this?"

She grinned. "Of course. And clearly keeping you busy worked. Happy Birthday, sweetheart!"

Tanner let that sink in, taking particular note of her term of endearment. "Thanks," he told her, then whispered in her ear, "I'm going to get you for this."

She chuckled, whispering back, "I'm counting on it."

"I could tell you to get a room," Solomon said with a laugh, "but I'm sure you already have that covered. Right now, it's all about celebrating your birthday among family, friends and employees."

Tanner would have preferred to celebrate his birthday with quiet reflection, if at all. But he knew this was Solomon's way of showing him love, and he wanted to go with the flow.

He smiled. "Thanks."

Solomon patted Tanner on the shoulder. "Good thing you're bald, big brother. Otherwise, I'm sure I would see a lot of gray hair up there, now that you're an old man."

Tanner glanced at his brother's dark hair, spotting a few gray strands beginning to sprout. "I wouldn't doubt it," he said, while noting that Melanie was not at his side. Was she somewhere in the crowd? Or had Solomon not invited her at all?

Imagining Bianca was thinking the same thing, Tanner took her hand and made their way into the gathering.

Frank gave him a stiff handshake and a glass of champagne. "Don't drink it all at once," he said teasingly.

"I don't intend to," Tanner promised, taking a sip as another glass was handed to Bianca. "I suppose you were in on this, too?"

Frank played dumb for a moment and then responded, "We wanted to do something special for the brains behind this magnificent hotel and casino."

"And it looks like you pulled it off without a hitch," Tanner said with a grin.

"At least, we wanted to make it look that way when all was said and done," Frank told him, laughing.

Tanner didn't doubt that it took a coordinated effort to plan this while keeping him in the dark. He applauded all for the effort, including Bianca, who'd played her role to perfection.

Kendre Kelly approached them wearing one of her stunning and provocative stage outfits. In her best imitation of Marilyn Monroe singing for President John F. Kennedy, Kendre sang "Happy Birthday" to Tanner.

"Thanks, I appreciate that," he told her, a little bashfully.

She tiptoed and kissed his cheek. "Hope you have many more birthdays to celebrate."

Tanner colored. "You and me both."

Kendre touched Bianca's arm and cooed, "Better hang on to this one. A lot of girls in this town would love to be where you are."

"I intend to do just that," Bianca told her confidently, slipping her arm around Tanner's waist. "He is a special guy."

Kendre winked at him and sashayed away.

"Better watch out for that one," Bianca whispered.

Tanner wondered if she was actually jealous. "Oh, she's just being naturally flirtatious," he said casually. "Don't let it get you bent out of shape."

"I'm not jealous, if that's what you're thinking."

"Good to know, because Kendre can't hold a candle to you."

"Oh, really?" Bianca tilted her head.

"Yes, really," Tanner stated, gazing at her face. "Don't you know just how gorgeous you are?"

She flushed. "I have some idea, but it's still nice to hear it from your lips."

"Then you'll keep hearing it," he promised.

"Hey, birthday boy!" Chuck said, walking up to them.

"Hey," Tanner said back.

Chuck shook his hand and gave him a little hug. "Would've been here sooner, but couldn't break away from a meeting with a client."

"Not a problem." Tanner smiled at him understandingly. "Glad you could come."

"Wouldn't have missed it."

Tanner looked at Bianca and said, "This is a good friend of mine, Chuck Newman. Chuck, this is Bianca, my girlfriend."

Chuck grinned as he shook her hand. "Nice to finally meet the person Tanner has been drooling over. And I can certainly see why."

She flashed her teeth at him. "Nice to meet you, too."

"Where's Deloris?" Tanner asked, adding for Bianca, "His wife..."

Chuck frowned. "I came right from the office. The four of us are still on for dinner next week, right?"

"Yeah," Tanner said.

"Great. Deloris is looking forward to meeting you, Bianca."

"I look forward to meeting her, too," she responded cheerfully.

Tanner smiled, glad to have Bianca meet the other people who were important in his life. He had no doubt that she and Deloris would get along great, even if he hadn't had a chance before now to tell her about their dinner plans.

After an hour or so more of mingling at the birthday bash, Tanner managed to quietly slip away with Bianca back to his hotel suite.

They wasted little time getting undressed and into bed. Bianca couldn't think of a better birthday present for Tanner than to make love and keep him wanting more.

She lay on her side with her back against his hard chest and stomach as he entered her. Bianca gasped as she felt his manhood inside the condom impale her. She gripped it tightly, drawing him in deeper, exciting her to no end.

Leaning her head back, Bianca found Tanner's mouth and they began to kiss deeply. With nimble fingers, he stroked her clitoris simultaneously with the sex that connected their bodies.

"Oh…Tanner," she cooed through his mouth as the powerful sensations of his stimulation and sexual prowess made her very wet and unable to prevent herself from coming in waves.

Tanner held her as she shook violently from the onslaught of satisfaction. No man had ever before been able to light her fire the way he did, making Bianca all the more delirious in expressing her orgasmic release.

She sucked in a deep breath, and then accommodated him, raising her leg as Tanner tucked beneath it, changing their position. He got on top of her, fitting himself between her thighs. Bianca bent her knees and clasped his hands over her head as Tanner thrust himself into her like a man obsessed.

She arched her back gleefully, caught up in the intensity of the moment.

By the time Tanner reached his orgasm, Bianca had found a second one, more potent than the first. Their perspiring bodies rocked the bed back and forth, and the mutual gratification left them prisoners of their lust for each other and the joy it brought.

Afterward, Bianca cradled Tanner's head against her breasts as they lay naked and caught their breaths. The intoxicating scent of their sex permeated the air.

"That was one hell of a birthday gift!" Tanner said with a chuckle.

"For me as much as you," Bianca confessed shamelessly.

"I always did believe that it was just as nice to give as to receive."

Bianca smiled. "I hope you never stop believing that," she uttered. *And I hope that I continue to be the object of your giving in bed for some time to come,* she thought.

Tanner kissed her breast. "I won't," he promised. "Not when I can get so much back in return."

"I try my best," she said, taking that as a compliment.

"And your best is more than good enough."

"You think?"

"You've proven it time and time again," Tanner said. "I don't want to lose what we have."

She pressed her lips to his head thoughtfully. "Neither do I," she admitted. But would that be enough to keep them together?

Bianca preferred not to go there. She'd much rather bask in their intimate connection and the bond that seemed to be growing between them with each and every day.

# Chapter 14

The next morning, Tanner found Solomon in the fitness center lifting weights.

"You're up early," Tanner commented.

"So are you...considering you left the birthday party with your lady," Solomon said.

Tanner chuckled. "She had to go to work—and so did I."

"Yeah, I hear you."

"Maybe next time I'll throw you a birthday bash."

"I'm all for a good time," Solomon said.

"Is that why you seem so glum?" Tanner asked.

"Who says I'm glum?"

"I could tell yesterday, but didn't say anything," Tanner said as he grabbed some weights. "I noticed Melanie wasn't in the ballroom."

"I didn't invite her," Solomon muttered.

"Why not?" Tanner figured he was entitled to ask, even if it was none of his business.

Solomon took a breath. "It's over between us."

"Oh." Tanner favored him with a bleak stare. "Who dumped whom?"

"I dumped her, if you want to call it that."

"What would you call it?"

Solomon wiped sweat from his brow. "I'd call it just deciding it was time to move on. We were starting to get on each other's case too much. It wasn't fun anymore."

"It's not always going to be fun and games in a relationship," Tanner said. "Sometimes you have to make adjustments along the way."

Solomon looked at him. "Are you talking about me or you—"

"Maybe both of us," admitted Tanner. "I just don't want to see you lose something that seemed to be working for you."

Solomon furrowed his brow. "But that's the thing— it stopped working, so I ended it before things got any worse."

Tanner couldn't fault him for getting out of a relationship that was apparently going nowhere. Why drag it out, if the end was inevitable? Or had Solomon simply gotten cold feet at the first sign that he was really starting to feel something for someone?

"Every time I see you with Bianca, it looks like things are solid between you guys. Is that how it is?" Solomon asked, lifting a weight.

"I don't have any complaints," Tanner told him. "Neither does she, as far as I know."

"Glad to hear that. Sounds like you're serious about her, and vice versa."

Tanner shrugged. "We haven't looked too far ahead."

He started to run in place pensively. "But, yes, I like what she brings to the table."

"And obviously she likes what you bring to the table," Solomon said. "Just be careful, big brother. I don't want you to get over your head and end up—"

"Falling in love?" Tanner asked.

"I'm not saying it's the worst thing in the world, but it's easy for women to latch on to us for all the wrong reasons."

Tanner's brows touched each other. "Bianca's not that type of person," he stressed.

"If not, then you're in no hurry to get hitched, if that is what this is leading up to."

"It's not," Tanner told him. "Marriage is certainly not at the top of my list in life at the moment."

Solomon smiled. "Good. Mine, either. Right now, I just want to be with someone fun and fine—minus the drama."

Tanner grinned. He had no issue with a little drama, if only to keep things lively. He got a lively lady for sure with Bianca—both in and out of bed. He could see himself falling in love and marrying her one day, if things continued to move in the right direction for them.

But first, he suspected he would have to deal with the breakup between Solomon and Melanie.

Bianca found Melanie in the lunchroom at work. She was sitting alone and her eyes were red, as if she'd been crying.

"What's wrong?" Bianca asked, suspecting it had something to do with Solomon. After all, she hadn't seen Melanie at the party yesterday with him.

"Solomon broke up with me," she said dejectedly.

Bianca lifted a brow. "Why?"

Melanie rolled her eyes. "Same old, same old for men—run away when things gets a little dicey."

"What do you mean by a little dicey?" Bianca asked.

"I just wanted a stable relationship with a good man," Melanie responded. "I thought Solomon was that man. But apparently he was more interested in friendship with benefits until someone better came along."

Bianca met her eyes. "Is there someone else?"

"I have no idea," Melanie moaned. "But it wouldn't surprise me. Isn't that what most men do…play women against each other? Especially when they're spoiled, rich bachelors."

If that was true, Bianca couldn't help but wonder if she was headed down the same path with Tanner. Or was she jumping the gun in comparing the brothers?

"Maybe you should talk to Solomon," she suggested.

Melanie sneered. "And say what? Please take me back and you can do anything you want, with anyone? I don't think so. I'm not *that* desperate."

"I wasn't implying that," Bianca told her. "All I'm saying is that some things are worth holding on to. Sometimes talking things through can get you back on track."

"If Solomon wants to get us back on track, he has my number," Melanie snorted.

Feeling the need, Blanca gave her a hug. "I'm sorry about this."

"Don't be—it happens. I'll get over it, in time." Melanie looked up at her. "I know you've said things are great between you and Tanner, but if I were you, I wouldn't get too comfortable in that relationship. He and Solomon are cut from the same cloth. They are used to getting what they want from whom they want. It may just be a matter of time before Tanner also decides that you're getting too close for comfort and it's time to cut you loose."

"He's not like that," Bianca said, and tried to convince herself at the same time.

Melanie batted her lashes skeptically. "Uh-huh. We'll see."

Bianca wrinkled her nose. "Look, I wish things had worked out for you and Solomon, but please don't try and make out like he and Tanner are clones of each other. I know Tanner truly cares about me."

"I never said he didn't," Melanie claimed.

"So what are you saying?" Bianca demanded.

Melanie paused. "Only that I hope you aren't as unlucky as I seem to be in this town, that's all. If Tanner is your pot of gold, then I'm truly happy for you. If he doesn't turn out to be, I'm there for you."

"Thanks," Bianca said weakly. She welcomed the support, but hoped she didn't need it as far as Tanner was concerned. It seemed as if things were progressing nicely between them on a daily basis. But would that come to a grinding halt out of the blue? Would she wake up one morning and find that her charming handsome prince had turned into a frog?

"We've got some high rollers coming in from Japan on Thursday," Frank informed Tanner as they walked around the casino.

"Great," Tanner told him. "You can comp their rooms and do whatever you can to make them feel right at home at the Aloha Seas."

"Will do," Frank said. "We also have two conventions and a trade show coming up next month."

"Sounds like the place will be rocking," Tanner told him.

"That's the name of the game," Frank said. "The more business we can line up, the less there will be for our competitors."

Tanner smiled. "I like the way you think. No wonder I brought you in as general manager."

Frank chuckled. "And to think, I thought it was all because of my ability to charm the ladies."

"That, too," Tanner said with a laugh.

"Speaking of that, Solomon told me he's back in the market for female companionship."

"Yeah, I heard." Tanner wondered if he'd truly ever been out of the market in the first place.

"Guess, when you've got it all, it's hard to know who to share it with," Frank suggested.

"I'm not so sure about that," Tanner said, glancing at some gamblers playing the slot machines as though their very lives depended on it. "Firstly, no one has it all. Secondly, you can't take it with you, so if you can find someone to share it with, take a chance and go for it."

"Good points." Frank regarded him. "Is that what you're doing with your lady friend—taking a chance and going for it?"

"Something like that," Tanner answered thoughtfully. "In her case, I consider the risks low and the gains incredibly high."

Frank smiled. "Those are odds I like."

"Me, too," Tanner said with a grin. He hoped those odds worked in Bianca's favor, too, in choosing him to give her affections to and, just maybe, her heart.

Bianca made Tanner dinner that night and then they made love. It was terrific as always, leaving her feeling satisfied and yearning for more. But she was also troubled by the way things had ended between Melanie and Solomon and what it could mean, if anything, for her relationship with Tanner.

They were still cuddling, enjoying the sweet aftermath of their sex, when Bianca commented, "Were you ever going to tell me that things were over between Solomon and Melanie?"

"I figured Melanie would tell you that," Tanner said evenly.

"She did," Bianca admitted. "I just thought—"

"That I would interject myself into my brother's love life?"

"I never wanted you to do that."

"I could say the same thing about Melanie," he said. "That's between her and Solomon."

"Is it…?" Bianca looked up at him.

"What's that supposed to mean?"

She took a breath and decided to speak her mind. "Well, given the way he just basically kicked her to the curb, I couldn't help but wonder if I might suffer the same fate…"

"First of all, I could just as easily be kicked to the curb, as you say, by you," Tanner said irritably. "That's the way it goes sometimes in relationships, whether we like it or not. That said, I'm not my brother, okay?" He gave her a steady look. "And you sure as hell are not Melanie. That's not a knock against her at all. What I'm trying to say is that how I feel about you is based entirely on what I want in a woman. It has nothing to do with Solomon's comings and goings."

Bianca took his point regarding relationship breakups that happened all the time. Still, she felt comforted in hearing his words. "So, exactly what is it you want in a woman?"

He held her a little tighter. "Just what I have in you," he said concisely.

"Which is?" she asked, needing to hear the words.

"All the things that make you who you are."

"Nice answer." Even if she wanted more details, Bianca wouldn't rock the boat by demanding them. When he had more to say, she was sure he would. In fact, she was counting on it.

"I could ask you the same question," Tanner said. "Why are you with me, putting aside my money and good looks?"

Bianca couldn't help but laugh. "What other reason would there be?" she tossed back playfully.

"You tell me."

"All right," she said in earnest. "Your attractiveness is definitely a positive. Your money is yours and isn't at all why I'm with you. I've never been rich and don't need to be rich. What I do need is a strong and confident man, one who exudes sexuality, intelligence and sensitivity, and one who doesn't always take life too seriously. Oh, and being a great cook certainly helps, too." Bianca met his eyes. "You possess all those qualities. Need I say more?"

He grinned. "No, you need not."

She smiled back, running her hand between his legs. "Then what do you say we table all this talk and let our actions take over?"

"I'd say you're on."

Bianca grabbed his erection. "I'd say you're on, too."

He chuckled. "And whose fault is that?"

"Umm… I'll take the Fifth…"

Tanner ran his thumb across her nipple before kissing it. "And I'll take you."

"Please do," Bianca uttered.

She felt as aroused as he was, while grateful that Tanner wasn't Solomon and that there was still a bright future to look forward to. And she intended to do just that.

# Chapter 15

The couples came together in Kula's, the Aloha Seas' Polynesian restaurant.

Bianca was happy to spend time with Tanner's friends, and they seemed just as comfortable around her. She wanted to be a part of his life in every way that was important and hoped he felt the same. For now, she was content to let things play out as they were between them and see which doors they chose to walk through.

She ate and listened as Chuck's pretty Asian wife, Deloris, talked animatedly about her husband and Tanner's long friendship.

"When I first began dating Chuck," she said, "I practically thought I needed to ask Tanner's permission, they were so tight."

Tanner threw his head back with laughter. "Funny, but Chuck's always been his own man. He saw someone who captured his fancy and didn't hold back."

Chuck laughed while holding his wineglass. "I think I can say the same thing about you, old buddy." He favored Bianca with an even gaze. "Looks to me like you've found someone who really works for you, and I couldn't be happier for you."

"Neither could I," Tanner stressed, turning to Bianca. "And, yes, she works for me on many levels."

Bianca took that in gleefully, while nibbling at her food. "I can say the same thing about you," she freely admitted.

"Thank you!" Tanner beamed and tilted his head to give her a kiss.

"We get it!" Chuck said. "Save that for later. We certainly intend to." He turned to kiss his wife.

"Some things just can't be helped," Tanner declared.

Bianca warmed at the thought of his kind words, often backed up with affection and attention. They did seem to be a match made in heaven. Or would it be best to remain earthbound, for now, in assessing where they were in the relationship?

"How did you two meet?" Deloris asked curiously, regarding Bianca.

Chuck grinned. "It was straight out of a Hollywood movie, but certainly not scripted."

Bianca smiled and recited the tale that seemed almost surreal as she looked back. She wondered if there truly were forces at work in the universe that somehow made it all possible.

"That's a sweet story," Deloris said. "Maybe it'll have a Hollywood ending, too."

"Never say never," Tanner said, sipping his wine.

Bianca was speechless. She didn't necessarily believe in Hollywood endings that were, after all, fake. However, she did hope to have a real-life ending with Tanner—a lifelong relationship and whatever that entailed.

"I was a showgirl when Chuck and I met," Deloris said, surprising Bianca.

"Oh, really?" she asked, picturing Deloris in an elaborate costume, performing.

"Yes. I guess I left quite an impression on him, and vice versa, before we fell in love and married."

"That's wonderful," Bianca said. She recalled when lovely showgirls surrounded Tanner during his grand-opening speech. At the time, he seemed right at home with the company. Did at least part of him wish she were an entertainer instead of someone who reported about entertainment in the city? Could she continue to keep his interest in the face of the beautiful women who were always around?

"It's the stuff Vegas is known for," Tanner said, sitting back in his chair. "It brings people together from all walks of life."

"Believe me, it works!" Chuck declared. "And evidently it's working for you two, as well."

"Hear, hear!" Tanner grinned and held up his drink, which Chuck clicked joyously.

"Hear, hear." Deloris followed.

"Definitely!" Bianca smiled and clinked wineglasses with Deloris before doing the same with Tanner. His eyes burned into her soul, and she felt like kissing him for the special man he was.

Following her instincts, Bianca did just that, tasting the wine in his kiss, which turned her on that much more. When she pulled away to quell her libido, she read the raw desire in Tanner's eyes. It, too, diminished in the present company, but would undoubtedly return in full force once they were behind closed doors.

Until then, she was more than happy to enjoy his company and that of his friends.

A week later, Bianca was at her desk at work when Leslie walked up to her.

"I just set up an interview for you with Kendre Kelly," her boss said.

Bianca reacted. "Really?"

"Yes. As one of the hottest acts in Vegas, if not the world, these days, what she has to say will sell papers."

"I understand," Bianca said thoughtfully. "Actually, I've already met Kendre, so it should be interesting to interview her."

Leslie smiled. "Good. She's willing to squeeze you in between sets at the Aloha Seas this afternoon."

"I'll be there," Bianca said, knowing it would also give her another excuse to visit Tanner. As if she needed one.

At one o'clock she was knocking on Kendre's dressing room door.

"Come in," she yelled.

Bianca went inside and found Kendre sitting at her makeup table, applying lip gloss.

"Hi," Bianca said nervously.

"Hey." Kendre flashed a surprised look. "I know the editor said Bianca Wagner would be doing the interview, but I didn't put two and two together...."

"You had no reason to," Bianca said, knowing she had never been identified to Kendre by her last name.

"True. Have a seat."

Bianca sat in a chair close to Kendre's and picked up the scent of her flowery perfume. "Thanks for doing an interview. I know you have a busy schedule," Bianca said as she took out her notepad.

"Happy to do so—for my career, the Aloha Seas and even you," Kendre said, and brushed her hair. "How long have you worked for the *Vegas Valley Happenings?*"

"Too long," Bianca answered indirectly. "Or so it seems, sometimes."

"I know what you mean. I've been singing professionally since I was twelve years old. Feels like forever."

"It shows that you've got staying power," Bianca told her, knowing how many singers burned out after only a few years.

"And an entourage who depend on me to keep this up for as long as I can," Kendre said.

This didn't surprise Bianca, given that most people in the entertainment business were codependent on the various hangers-on and other enablers.

"The way you sing, it could be a quite a while before you're ready to slow down."

Kendre smiled. "Thanks." She sat back in her chair, studying Bianca. "Being an entertainment reporter is your day job?"

"Yes, you could say that," Bianca said. "Sometimes my night job, too."

"I thought the nights might be devoted to spending time with Tanner," Kendre remarked with a catch to her voice.

Bianca smiled. "We have our time together in the day and night."

"So, he's pretty good in bed?"

Bianca's cheeks rose. She wasn't sure she wanted to talk about their sex life. But she did want to keep it casual, so Kendre would open up more about herself.

"Yes, he's pretty hot in and out of bed," she told her.

Kendre grinned. "I'll bet. And the way he has his

eye on you, I'm guessing that he feels the same way about you."

"I'd like to think so," admitted Bianca.

"Tanner reminds me of my last boyfriend," Kendre remarked. "Or, actually, the one before last. He was all that, but was too interested in other ladies, as well."

"Sorry to hear that." Bianca looked at her while wishing it hadn't been Tanner who reminded Kendre of her last boyfriend.

"No big deal. I'm so over him."

"Good, because there are so many hot guys out there—especially in Vegas," Bianca decided to say.

"Too many, really," Kendre said. "I just wish I had the time to go after some of them. But my plate's pretty full these days with the music."

"Well, you're still young, so there's lots of time to do the romance thing when it's right for you."

"Yeah, you're right. Maybe then I'll get lucky like you and strike gold."

Bianca flashed a half smile, finding it hard to believe someone so successful would be envious of her, as Kendre seemed to be. "I'm not sure I'd exactly say I've struck gold with Tanner," she said. "There's lots of fool's gold out there. Tanner and I know we have a good thing in each other and are just letting the chips fall where they may, if I may use a gambling analogy."

Kendre laughed. "Why not? It's certainly most appropriate in this town."

"True." Bianca laughed with her and used this moment to redirect the interview. "So, who was your inspiration to become a singer?"

Kendre stared at the question thoughtfully. "All the great ladies of song that came before me," she said. "Including my mother, who sang in the choir and encouraged me from the very beginning to use the voice I'd been given."

Bianca jotted this down. "Your mother deserves a lot of credit for where you are today?"

"Yes, definitely. I don't know how far I would've gotten without her. My father has also been my rock. But mostly it's hard work and getting the right breaks along the way that have led to my success and being the first singer to be booked at Aloha Seas!"

"From what I've seen and heard, Tanner made a great choice with you," Bianca told her.

Kendre smiled and said while eyeing her, "Funny, I was thinking the same thing about you."

Bianca cocked a brow while allowing that to sink in. Had others been talking about her involvement with Tanner?

Either way, Bianca decided that there was no harm in being the envy of Kendre or anyone else. Having Tanner was a great thing, and she wouldn't apologize for it. Or move aside for anyone else to come swooping in to claim her man.

## Chapter 16

Tanner was thrilled when Bianca agreed to work out with him at the fitness center. She was in excellent shape, as was he, and it showed as she moved her toned arms and legs gracefully on an elliptical machine. He imagined those long, shapely legs wrapped around his waist as they made love.

The thought aroused him and he had to turn his thoughts off, realizing it wasn't the time or place. Still, it only reinforced the strong feelings he had for her. He was sure she felt the same way.

"I interviewed Kendre Kelly today," Bianca tossed out as she took a break and sipped some bottled water.

"I know," Tanner told her nonchalantly, wiping his glistening brow with a towel.

"Really?" She regarded him with surprise.

"Yeah, I ran into Kendre in the lobby," he said. "She mentioned that she'd given you an exclusive."

"I see," Bianca muttered.

Tanner cocked a brow. "What do you see?"

Bianca's eyes expanded. "I see that she wants you."

"What?" He bristled.

"You heard me. The lady wants to get in your pants."

Tanner rolled his eyes. "Not this again." He recalled the last time she had decided the singing sensation was after him.

"Yes, this again," Bianca retorted. "You remind Kendre of one of her last boyfriends and what she's missing."

He laughed while moving on the elliptical machine. "I'm flattered, but that hardly means she wants to be with me—"

"Think whatever you want, but I'm just telling it like I see it. She's a fabulous singer—even if she did a terrible impression of Marilyn Monroe on your birthday—but she's also lonely and dreaming of getting lucky with you."

"Well, it's not going to happen, assuming that's true."

"Not as long as we're together," Bianca stressed.

"Or even after." Tanner gazed at her. "I'm not in the slightest bit interested in Kendre Kelly, aside from what she can do to bring visitors to the Aloha Seas. Okay?"

"If you say so."

"I do say so. Nothing to get jealous over."

"I'm not jealous," Bianca stated. "Just perceptive."

"Yeah, right." Tanner smiled thinly.

"Seriously," Bianca said. "I only mentioned it so you could be on guard. It doesn't mean I can't handle other women lusting for your body."

He cracked a grin as she gave him the once-over. He was shirtless and wore only gray compression shorts. It was obvious to him that she liked everything she saw. "You sure about that?"

"Yes, but it doesn't mean I have to like it."

Tanner had to admit that he was less than thrilled, as well, with men wanting her, even if they had no chance of having her. He was also realistic enough to know that it came with the territory when you were seeing a beautiful and sexy woman. Just as Bianca had to know, as well, that given his good looks and great success in that town, it made it easy for other women to desire him sexually or otherwise.

He got off the elliptical machine and grabbed her waist. "I'm guilty of lusting after you," he said sexily. "So what do you say we do something about it?"

She wrinkled her nose. "But we're all sweaty and smelly."

"What do you think we'll be while we're having hot sex?" he asked squarely, aroused at the thought. "This will just give us a head start."

Bianca laughed. "You're really naughty."

"And you aren't?"

He didn't give her time to respond, laying a big kiss on her lips as a prelude to things to come.

Bianca had no problem putting Kendre Kelly out of her thoughts as Tanner gave her his full and thorough attention, making love to her with the same type of energy and passion that he had shown previously. It left her breathless, even while she matched him step for step in wanting to make the experience every bit as pleasurable for him.

Once their heart rates and bodies had calmed down, Bianca wanted to jump into the shower and took Tanner with her.

They soaped and rinsed each other, kissed, and enjoyed the contact and nonverbal communication.

Afterward, they sat in the living room enjoying a glass of wine.

"Am I ever going to meet your sister?" Tanner asked.

Bianca looked at him. "Where did that come from?"

"I've been thinking about it for a while now," he said. "You've met my brother, and since you've mentioned that you and your sister are tight, I thought it would be nice if I got to meet her and your brother-in-law, face-to-face."

Bianca hadn't realized he was interested. It pleased her that he was, which suggested that he cared enough about her to want to get close to Madison and Stuart.

"I'd be happy to invite them," she said.

Tanner smiled. "Why don't you? I can comp them a suite here. We can take in a show and just shoot the breeze."

"That's so sweet of you, but I'm sure they can pay for their room—"

"I'm sure they can, too," Tanner said. "But why should they, when your boyfriend owns a hotel and casino?"

"So you want to impress them?" Bianca asked.

"No, I just want to make your sister and brother-in-law feel at home in Vegas," he insisted. "The best way I can do that is to invite them into my home, so to speak. When we go to Portland, they can put us up, if they like."

Bianca smiled at the thought. "So you're already planning to visit the Rose City?" *With me?*

Tanner grinned as he tasted more wine. "Sure, why not? Family is important to me. And that's where your family lives. I'd like to be connected to them."

"I'd like that, too," she told him. "And I'd love to visit Portland with you."

"Then it's settled. First, you invite them to Vegas, and we'll go from there."

"Sounds like a plan." Bianca relished the thought of introducing the man in her life to her sister, knowing Madison would jump at the chance to return to Las Vegas. It also served as an indicator that Tanner was as serious about their relationship as she was, making Bianca feel that he really was the right man for her.

That evening she gave Madison a call, eager to share the news of their possible reunion.

"Hey, you," Madison said cheerfully.

"Hey." Bianca propped her head up on her pillow. "Busy?"

"Not at all. The girls are asleep and Stuart has buried himself in his office while he tries to beat the deadline on his latest novel."

"I don't doubt that it's hard work, since I have my own deadlines to meet at the paper."

"Speaking of, I meant to thank you for emailing me the copy of the story you did on Tanner," Madison said. "The cover photo was nice, too."

"Well, I can't take credit for the photograph," Bianca joked. "As for the photographer, having something to work with always helps."

Madison laughed. "That's for sure. In this case, Tanner has more than enough going on in that department."

"As does Stuart," Bianca said, feeling that her sister couldn't have chosen a nicer-looking guy in all of Portland.

"I'll be sure to let him know you said that," Madison said. "He'll get a kick out of it."

"I have a better idea." Bianca paused. "Why not let me tell him in person?"

"You're coming here?"

"Actually, Tanner and I would like to invite you to come here for a couple of days," Bianca told her. "You'd stay in a suite at the Aloha Seas, free of charge."

"Wow!" Madison exclaimed enthusiastically. "When?"

"Whenever you can come. I was thinking you could leave the girls with a babysitter. Or you can even bring them, if you like."

"It's probably best that they stay home with a nanny while we visit," Madison said. "Maybe when they're older—"

"Absolutely!" Bianca said, thinking positively that there would be a next time, and that she and Tanner would still be an item.

"I'll check with Stuart, but I'm sure he'll be up for a little getaway after he sends this book off."

"Cool."

"I know I could use a vacation," Madison told her.

"Yeah, me too." Bianca imagined going somewhere exotic with Tanner someday.

"So, things must be getting pretty serious between you and Tanner if you're inviting us to hang out with you in Vegas."

"Yes, I believe they are," Bianca admitted. "The truth is that it was Tanner's suggestion that I invite you here. He wants to meet my sister."

"Oh…how sweet," Madison said. "Well, I can't wait to meet him, either. I'm sure Stuart will feel the same way, knowing that Tanner makes you happy."

Bianca smiled. "He does."

"Then I'm happy for you."

"Thanks. I'm not where you are yet in a relationship, but we seem to really click."

"More than with other men you've dated?"

Bianca sighed. "I know I don't have the best track record, but this one is different."

"He must be," Madison said. "I can hear it in your voice."

"Can you?" Bianca couldn't help but blush.

"Yes. You are hooked, girl!"

Bianca laughed. "I think I am," she admitted.

"Will wonders never cease," Madison said light-heartedly. "My big sister seems to have finally landed a big fish!"

"This isn't about fish," Bianca stressed. "Tanner is very down-to-earth, and we *get* each other."

"I believe you. Of course, I'll get to judge for myself amidst the splendor of his hotel-casino."

"Wouldn't have it any other way, Judge Madison," Bianca joked.

Madison chuckled. "All in all, it sounds like a terrific idea and lots of fun."

"Count on it."

Bianca was a trifle nervous about her boyfriend and sister sizing each other up like gladiators, but she was sure they would get along well. As would Tanner and Stuart.

Bianca hoped Tanner would eventually get to meet her darling little nieces, perhaps when they took a trip to Portland. While there, they could even take a side trip to the coast or the mountains. He seemed perfectly amenable to the idea, which, in and of itself, told Bianca that Tanner really was all about family. That gave her a warm feeling inside and the genuine belief that things could be heading in the direction where they might one day have a family of their own.

It was a thought Bianca rested on.

## Chapter 17

Tanner watched with amusement as Solomon appeared to be putting the moves on a striking tall blonde in the casino.

When Solomon saw his brother, he whispered something to the woman and sent her on her way.

"Didn't mean to interrupt anything," Tanner said.

"You weren't," Solomon responded. "She's just a blackjack dealer I was giving a few pointers to."

Tanner rolled his eyes. "Yeah, right. Since when did you become an expert on dealing cards?"

Solomon kept a straight face. "I'm not trying to get into her pants. We're cool, strictly on a professional level."

"If you say so." Tanner gave him the benefit of the doubt, but was sure that it wouldn't be long before his brother had found a new woman to cozy up to—before finding an excuse to move on to someone else.

They headed away from the casino.

"Speaking of ladies, when is Bianca's sister coming?" Solomon asked.

"Tomorrow," Tanner said, thinking about it with anticipation. It wasn't so much that he wanted to impress Madison, per se. He just wanted to get to know the sister of the woman he was so hung up on. And, more importantly, he wanted her to get to know who he was beyond the facade and CEO tag.

"Is she as gorgeous as Bianca?" Solomon asked.

Tanner detected a glint in his brother's eye at the prospect of hooking up with her. "From a picture I saw, she's every bit as gorgeous. She's also happily married with two children."

Solomon frowned. "Well, good for her."

*And her husband,* thought Tanner. "Maybe you should try it sometime," he said, "and you may be happy, too."

"Who says I'm not happy?"

"I'm sure you are, in your own way, but having someone to balance your life can make you happier," Tanner told him.

Solomon eyed him. "You mean, like Bianca?"

"Exactly."

"So, why not marry the lady who gives you balance, big brother? I'll even be your best man if you want."

Tanner nodded pensively. "I'm not at that point yet," he said honestly. "We'll see how it goes. But that doesn't mean I think any less of Bianca. Quite the contrary. I probably think more of her than I have any other woman I've dated."

"Hmm...sounds like the big *L* word to me," Solomon said.

"Let's just say I'm headed in the right direction

there," Tanner responded, scratching his chin. "But I'd rather not get ahead of myself. We need to continue to dot the *i*'s and cross the *t*'s in this relationship, until we both know without question that it's right."

"Understood." Solomon chuckled. "You always were the analytical one of the family."

"And you were the most impulsive," Tanner said with a smile.

"Guess that's why we make such a good team in business," Solomon said. "It's that balance thing again—like with you and Bianca."

"Yeah." Tanner gave a thoughtful nod as his mind moved to Bianca and the marvelous ways in which she had opened his eyes. He could only wonder what other things might be in store for them as their romance continued to blossom.

Bianca stood nervously in the lobby, trying not to shake as she held Tanner's hand and waited for Madison and Stuart to come through the doors. Tanner's driver, having picked them up from the airport, had phoned to announce that they'd arrived.

"This should be fun," Tanner told her, grinning confidently.

"You think so?" she asked, looking up at him.

"Yeah. That's what the Aloha Seas is all about. Together, we'll make sure your sister and brother-in-law leave here feeling like it's a place they can't wait to get back to."

Bianca smiled. "I like the way you think."

His eyes crinkled. "I feel the same way about you," he told her.

"Oh, there they are." She smiled as Madison and Stuart approached. A bellhop followed with their bags.

"Hey, sis," Madison said gleefully, and gave Bianca a hug.

*"Aloha!"* Bianca said. "Welcome to the closest thing to Hawaii you'll find on the mainland."

"I can see that. Can't wait to take in the luau."

"Hi," Bianca said to Stuart with a smile, glad she'd been able to pry him away from his writing.

"Hey," he said, grinning.

Bianca looked at Tanner. "This is my sister, Madison, and her husband, Stuart."

"I'm Tanner." He introduced himself. "Very nice to meet you both."

"Nice to meet you, too," Stuart said.

The two shook hands and then Tanner gave Madison a kiss on the cheek.

"Why don't Bianca and I show you to your suite and give you some time to freshen up," Tanner said. "Then we'll give you a tour of the hotel and casino, and grab a bite to eat."

"Sounds fantastic," Madison said.

"Yeah, that's great," seconded Stuart.

When they reached the suite, impressive all on its own, Bianca was surprised to see that a bottle of chardonnay and a basket of goodies were waiting, as well as flowers for Madison.

Madison put to her nose to the bouquet and declared, "It's lovely. Thank you."

Tanner smiled. "All part of the service at Aloha Seas for our special guests."

"Guess it pays to know people in high places," Stuart joked.

Bianca chuckled. "I'd say we're all in a pretty high place right now," she said, looking out the floor-to-ceiling window with its magnificent view of the Strip below.

"And since we all know each other now, it's all good," Tanner added lightheartedly.

Madison smiled, and Bianca knew that the ice had been broken, and now they could simply focus on catching up and having the time of their lives.

"Thanks for making them feel at home," Bianca said to Tanner after they had left Madison and Stuart alone to unpack and refresh.

"It was the least I could do to welcome them to my establishment," he responded smoothly.

"True, but now they might never want to leave," Bianca kidded.

"Then they don't have to." Tanner's eyes twinkled. "If keeping them here will make you happy, then I'm all for it."

Bianca melted to his words. "You're so sweet."

"Not half as sweet as you are." He tilted his face and gave her a stirring kiss that caused even Bianca's toes to tingle.

She pried their lips apart, licking hers. "Keep that up and we'll have to leave Madison and Stuart to be their own tour guides."

"Would that be so bad?"

"No," she admitted. "But it wouldn't exactly make us the perfect hosts if we were busy being intimate while the very people you invited here were left hanging."

"Good point." Tanner put his arm around her shoulders. "Guess we'll just have to suppress our desires till later."

"I guess so." Bianca knew it wasn't going to be easy, as she found herself craving his body all the time. She knew Tanner felt the same way, due to the insatiable drive that he demonstrated every chance they got to make love.

But the next couple of days were all about Madison and Stuart. Bianca was determined to take advantage of this time to bond with her sister and new brother-in-law, while also giving them the opportunity to get acquainted with the wonderful man in her life.

That evening, Tanner invited Madison and Stuart to his suite, along with Solomon, hoping to bring his family and Bianca's together. It seemed to be working like a charm as everyone sat around chatting amicably, including Solomon, who was on his best behavior and appeared to hit it off with Stuart and Madison.

"I actually saw the movie version of the book," Solomon said proudly of the screenplay adaptation of one of Stuart's bestsellers. "I thought it was great."

"I've heard that a lot," Stuart said. "Personally, I think that the book fleshes out the characters and plot much more."

"You would think that, Mr. Author," Madison said with a chuckle.

"I actually agree with Stuart," Bianca chipped in, while explaining that she had read this book and some of his other novels. "The movie doesn't really do the book justice."

"Maybe sometime we can talk about turning one of your other novels into a movie," Tanner suggested, surprising himself, as he had never particularly had an interest in producing movies. At the same time, he'd always been open to new money-making opportunities. "We could coproduce it. That way you could write the script yourself and tell the story the way you feel it should be told."

"Sounds interesting," Stuart said, sipping wine, "and something that could be worth pursuing."

"I might be interested in investing in that, as well, if it happens," Solomon said. "Could be a winning hand."

"I think we've created monsters with the three of them," Madison said lightheartedly.

"Or geniuses," Bianca suggested.

"I like being a genius better than a monster," Tanner proclaimed.

"Works for me, too," Stuart said.

"Yeah, same here," Solomon stated.

The three men toasted the notion.

Later, Bianca and Madison were alone on Tanner's private patio with its incredible view of Las Vegas.

"Was Tanner serious about working with Stuart to make a movie based on one of his novels?" Madison asked over her goblet of wine.

"Yes, I'm sure he was," Bianca told her, knowing that Tanner wasn't paying lip service simply to try to impress someone. She found the idea of their men and Solomon collaborating on a movie project appealing, even while wondering if it was a bit risky. She didn't doubt that Tanner had the resources to fund a motion picture, or even a television movie, knowing he was the type of man who was always looking for opportunities.

But she was somewhat leery about mixing business with her personal ties to Madison. They had reached a point in their lives where things were smooth between them, and Bianca didn't want anything to put that in jeopardy. "If you're uncomfortable with any of it—"

"No, I'm not," Madison said. "I saw the way Stuart's eyes lit up with the talk. He's long since felt that he could do a better job telling his stories in a feature, but hasn't had enough clout or money to make his voice heard once the rights to his books were sold."

Bianca smiled. "Well, maybe now he'll have enough of both to ensure things are done the correct way," she said.

Madison smiled. "Looks like you're doing things the correct way in finding a CEO at a first-rate hotel and casino on the Strip who seems to care a lot about you."

"Well, I didn't exactly seek Tanner out. Things just fell into place with us," Bianca pointed out, sipping her drink. "But we are trying to do this right, nonetheless, in terms of continuing to cultivate what we have and not trying to rush into anything."

Madison looked at her. "You mean like love…or marriage?"

"Both, though neither subject has ever been discussed," Bianca admitted.

"But you're at least thinking along those lines?"

"How could I not?" Sometimes it had been all she could think of, before getting a grip and containing her enthusiasm over the possibilities. "It still takes two to be in love and want marriage," she pointed out.

"So, you don't think Tanner feels the same way that you do?" Madison asked.

"I'm not sure he does," Bianca said. "For that matter, I'm not even sure how I feel along those lines."

"Maybe you need to find out before you get too emotionally invested in something that fizzles." Madison sighed. "I don't mean to suggest that he's just stringing you along—"

"I know," Bianca told her. "And you're right, we do need to discuss in more concrete terms where this relationship is going." Even if it only reached a certain point, such as where they were now, she wanted to know and deal with it.

"Could you be satisfied with what he offers you now?" Madison asked her. "Or, in other words, would you truly be happy being the girlfriend of a rich and very handsome mogul without a long-term commitment?"

Bianca sipped more wine as she mulled the question over. After a moment or two, she admitted, "I don't know. At first I thought I would. But the longer we are together, the more I feel like he is someone I could imagine spending the rest of my life with, but not necessarily as his girlfriend…"

"You might not have to," Madison said optimistically. "You haven't been dating that long. From my read of Tanner, he doesn't strike me as someone who's just keeping you around until someone better comes along."

"I agree," Bianca said, though she was mindful of Melanie's split with Solomon and her friend's implication that blood was thicker than water—that the brothers might be alike when it came to a love-them-and-leave-them attitude.

Bianca certainly didn't want to think that about Tanner, and he'd given her no reason to. But she couldn't let her guard down entirely. Otherwise, she could be setting herself up for something she wouldn't wish on anyone who was on the brink of falling in love.

The next day, Tanner agreed to hang out with Stuart while Bianca took Madison sightseeing and to have lunch with her friends.

Tanner was glad to learn that Stuart was into physical fitness almost as much as he was. It was another thing they had in common, besides being smitten with the two sisters.

They went to the fitness center and worked out.

"So, man to man, what can you tell me about Bianca that I might not already know?" Tanner decided to ask as he lifted weights.

Stuart, riding a stationary bike, considered the question. "Well, to tell you the truth, I don't really know Bianca all that well. But from what I do know, I'd say that she seems to be pretty independent and outspoken."

"Yeah, I gathered that much," Tanner said with amusement.

"She's also very protective of her sister. You should've seen the way she grilled me about my intentions with Madison when we first met," Stuart said. "I guess after Madison's previous boyfriend dumped her, Bianca wanted to be sure I wasn't going to pull the same stunt." He laughed. "I got the message loud and clear, and gained even more respect for Bianca and Madison in the process."

Tanner grinned. "So she's all about family loyalty and watching each other's backs?"

"Yeah, you could say that." Stuart slowed down on the bike for a moment. "I take it the same is true with you and your brother? I know it is for me and my sister."

"Definitely," Tanner said. He put down the weights and got on a treadmill.

"And what about you and Bianca?"

Tanner looked at him. "What about us?"

"Where do you see things going, if you don't mind my asking?"

"I don't mind," Tanner assured him and pondered his response. "As far as I'm concerned, I hope we can keep our relationship on the path it's headed down—wherever that leads us."

Stuart eyed him. "So marriage is not out of the question?"

Tanner paused. He didn't want to make any predictions. Or set himself—or her—up for failure. But he didn't want to sell their relationship short, either. Not the way he felt about Bianca.

"No, it's not," he answered candidly. "Of course, Bianca would have to feel the same way."

"Well, from what Madison has been saying, the lady's crazy about you," Stuart told him.

Tanner cocked a brow. "Is that what she said?"

"Came straight from the horse's mouth, so to speak." Stuart wiped perspiration from his face. "All I can say is that Bianca is stunning, just like Madison. If I were you, I would definitely hang on to her."

Tanner smiled. "I intend to do just that."

"And if we become brothers-in-law, I'd be cool with that, too," Stuart said, grinning.

"Yeah, that would be great," Tanner agreed. He loved his brother, but had no problem adding a brother-in-law. Along with a sister-in-law. But even if all that failed, he would settle for having some new friends. "In the meantime, we'll definitely have to keep in touch about possibly collaborating on a movie project."

Stuart grinned. "Absolutely."

Tanner got off the treadmill and wiped his face with a towel. "In fact, let's shower and then grab a bite to eat. I'll ask Solomon to meet us and we can talk some more about that."

"Good idea," Stuart agreed.

Tanner smiled while thinking that this could be a fringe benefit of his newfound camaraderie with Bianca's family. He imagined he could pitch the movie to some of his investors at the hotel-casino and get them interested. If everything worked out, he could add producer to his hat and use the power of the Aloha Seas to promote the movie.

Bianca, whom he most wanted to approve of this, could write about it for the newspaper and make it a true family affair. This was important to Tanner. After all, at the end of the day, what could be more important than family?

# Chapter 18

"This is so nice," Madison said as they watched Kendre Kelly leave the stage for a short break from her performance at the Aloha Seas.

Bianca, who was sitting next to Madison, smiled. "I agree. She's great!"

"And it's cool that you got to interview her."

"Just part of the job," Bianca said, trying to downplay it. Never mind that the singer had the hots for Bianca's boyfriend. But as long as Kendre kept her paws off him, Bianca had to stay away from becoming territorial when it came to Tanner. Just because many women, even famous ones, were attracted to him, didn't mean he would succumb to their charms. Not when Tanner had someone who adored him and, as far as she knew, kept him more than satisfied.

"Well, maybe we need to switch jobs," kidded Madison. "I love interviewing authors, but here in Vegas you get to interview everyone in the entertainment business."

"You could always move here." Bianca hugged her. "There's plenty of work in Vegas."

Madison laughed. "I don't think I'm cut out to be a showgirl or a stripper," she joked.

"Believe me, neither am I," Bianca said with a giggle. "Book reviewers, entertainment writers and such are always in demand here. I have a few contacts that I could always use to help the cause. And Stuart, as a self-employed writer, could work anywhere. It would be terrific if you and I could hang out together like when we were girls."

"Yes, that would be nice, but it wouldn't be a good idea to take the girls out of their school," Madison told her.

"You're right, of course." Bianca had to remember that when Madison married Stuart, it was a package deal that included the girls. Now Madison loved them as though they were her own. Bianca got to see firsthand what a great mother she was. *Will I be half as good a mother as Madison, someday?* she asked herself.

"Now, maybe one day when they are off to college, and Stuart and I are bored stiff, the lure of Las Vegas and my big sister might be too much to pass up."

Bianca chuckled. "I'll probably have a lot more gray hair by then and will likely have slowed down a bit, but you'll be more than welcome to come."

"Who knows, by that stage, you and your possible husband may have had a child or two of your own," suggested Madison, sipping her drink.

"Let's not get too far ahead of ourselves," Bianca warned, knowing that scenario—no matter how appealing—was too far off in the distance to even speculate on. "Right now, I'd like to focus on the here and now in my relationship with Tanner."

"I'm just saying...." Madison looked at her with bold eyes. "Maybe I've got a crystal ball that can see the future."

"Maybe I do, as well," Bianca countered. "I see a beautiful baby entering your picture so much sooner."

Madison laughed. "Really?"

"Yes. Why not? It's not like you aren't trying."

"Yes, I am— We are," Madison confirmed. "But so far, no luck."

"Well, that's why you're here in Vegas," Bianca said. "To enjoy some extra-special romance where luck has a strange habit of turning in your favor."

Madison grinned. "Spoken like the girlfriend of a rich hotel and casino owner."

Bianca chuckled. "And the sister of a devoted wife and mother whom I'm always looking after."

"That, too," Madison told her.

"As a bonus, I'll keep my fingers crossed that things work out for you and Stuart."

"Thanks, and I'll do the same for you and Tanner."

Bianca smiled, taking her words to heart.

They cut the conversation short when Kendre reappeared on stage to belt out another heartfelt song.

A week later, Tanner spent the night at Bianca's house. Neither of them got much sleep, but they both got lots of exercise.

This time, Bianca was making some old-fashioned pancakes when Tanner dragged himself out of bed, disappointed that she wasn't next to him. It was admittedly becoming a habit he didn't want to shake. And most of the time, neither did she.

Except when she sneaked out of bed to make breakfast for the both of them.

"Good morning, handsome," she said, handing him a cup of coffee.

"Good morning, beautiful," he told her. "You should have awakened me to help out."

"Just like you've done more than once at your place, right?" Bianca asked facetiously.

He laughed. "Point taken."

"Good. So have a seat and let me treat you like a king."

Tanner did just that in the breakfast nook and sipped the coffee, staring at Bianca's short robe. It turned him on. "I like being treated like a king by my queen."

"A queen, huh?" She eyed him while tossing a couple of pancakes onto a plate. "Is that what you want in a woman—a queen?"

He met her gaze. "What I want in a woman is you," he stated. "The queen part is a bonus."

Bianca smiled. "Do you have a book or website you study to know all the right things to say?"

Tanner chuckled. "It comes naturally."

"Then I'm certainly fortunate to be the one benefitting from your natural charm," she said, setting a plate before him.

"Actually, I'm the fortunate one to have you to dispense such genuine feelings to," he countered smoothly.

Bianca giggled. "You're too much."

"So are you." He poured syrup over his stack of pancakes. "On second thought, you're just right—beautiful, sexy and one hell of a woman."

"Hmm…" She leaned over him. "I think I know where this is headed after breakfast."

"It's nice to be on the same wavelength with someone," he said intimately, showing some restraint in not taking her right there.

"Yes, it is," she said, then took his fork and put a piece of pancake in her mouth, licking syrup off her lips seductively.

He laughed. "You're a bad girl."

"And you're a bad boy." She chuckled. "What a pair we make."

"You'll get no argument from me on that," he told her, gently squeezing Bianca's bottom before she went back to the griddle for her pancakes.

Half an hour later, Tanner's cell phone rang while they were still at the table. He could see it was from Frank and debated whether or not to call him back a little later.

"Take it," Bianca said. "I need to clean off the table, anyway."

"Okay." He clicked on the phone. "Yeah, Frank, what's up?"

When he disconnected, Tanner gave Bianca a thoughtful look.

"What is it?" she asked.

"How would you like to fly to London with me on Thursday?"

Bianca's eyes widened. "You mean London, England?"

"Yes. I have some business I need to attend to there on Friday morning," he told her. "After that, we can have the rest of the day and Saturday to ourselves before heading back."

"That's pretty short notice," she said.

"True, but it is an all-expense-paid trip to England on a private jet. You could call it a romantic getaway for us. Say you'll go."

Bianca took a moment to consider it before breaking

into a big smile. "I'll have to take a personal day from work, but, yes, I'd love to go."

Tanner smiled back. "Terrific. We'll make the most of it." Already, he found himself fantasizing about having sex with her thirty-thousand feet up in the air. And on the other side of the Atlantic.


Bianca sat in the coffee shop with Vicky on what had turned out to be a rainy afternoon.

"I can't believe you're going to London," Vicky said enviously.

"Neither can I, to tell you the truth," Bianca said, sipping coffee. It was the one place she had always wanted to go, but it had never been the right time. Until now.

"Obviously, Mr. Deep Pockets thinks you're pretty special to invite you."

"I think he's pretty special, too," Bianca admitted. "And it's not about his money. What Tanner brings to the table is more than all the money in the world."

Vicky laughed. "Listen to you."

"What?" Bianca's eyes widened as though dumbfounded.

"You sound very much like a woman in love—that's what."

"Maybe I am," Bianca suggested, even if not entirely comfortable with the prospect. After all, if he didn't feel the same way, then where did that leave her?

As though reading her, mind, Vicky asked, "Do you think he's in love with you, too?"

Bianca bit into a chocolate chip cookie as she mulled over the question. Was he?

"He acts like it, but—"

"But he hasn't said the words?" Vicky finished for her.

"Yes," Bianca acknowledged sadly. Not that she had come out and told him exactly how she felt, either. Were they both dodging the issue to protect themselves? Or did they not feel the same way at this stage of their relationship?

"Maybe that's what this trip is all about." Vicky speculated over her coffee cup. "Maybe the business trip part was just a trick to get you over there so he could declare his love and pop the question."

Bianca's brows lifted. "Are you crazy?" In her mind, it made little sense to travel halfway across the world to do what he could just as easily do in Las Vegas.

"I'm perfectly sane," Vicky said with a chuckle. "Think about it. What better place is there than London to ask you to marry him? It's one of the most romantic cities in the world."

"And Vegas isn't?" Bianca asked, rolling her eyes.

"Hey, not taking anything away from this town, but no, I don't honestly see Sin City as being all that romantic a setting for expressing your love, even with all the quick-marriage wedding chapels here. The marriages they perform are almost destined for failure."

Bianca laughed. "Since when did you become such an expert on love and marriage?"

"Since I fell in love with my boyfriend and he told me he feels the same," Vicky responded confidently.

"Why didn't you tell me?" Bianca asked, surprised.

"I'm telling you now, girlfriend." Vicky flashed her teeth. "And I'm also telling you that your day will come. Maybe sooner than you think…"

Bianca could only hope. She sipped her coffee thoughtfully as thoughts of Tanner filled her head, along with a renewed optimism for a bright future together.

## Chapter 19

Bianca sat cozily beside Tanner on a plush leather couch on his private jet as they cruised at an altitude of thirty-five thousand feet. It was her first time on a noncommercial plane, and it was something she could definitely get used to. *Who wouldn't want to jet around in this style if given the choice?* she asked herself. But she was more taken by being there with the man who was stealing her heart. The more she tried to keep from crossing that threshold, the more it became clear to Bianca that her feelings for Tanner were growing in leaps and bounds, and as far as she was concerned, there was no turning back.

"You're pretty quiet," Tanner said, breaking into her thoughts.

"Just relaxing and enjoying the flight," she told him, deciding now was not the right time to spring on him the fact that she was falling in love.

He grinned handsomely. "Well, I'm enjoying being with you on the flight," he said, handing her a cocktail.

Bianca smiled. "Same here." She took the glass and sipped the drink. "So, how long have you had your own plane?"

"About a year," he said. "I got a good deal on it."

"Everyone needs to be able to afford such good deals," she joked.

Tanner chuckled. "Yeah, I agree. I know it's just another trapping of great success, but you have to spend your money somehow, right?"

"Right," she said. "You've earned it. And if you don't spend it, who will?"

"My sentiments exactly."

Bianca looked at him curiously. "How many other women have you jetted off to Europe with?"

Tanner kept a straight face. "Do you really want to know?"

"Yes, that's why I asked," she said honestly.

"Okay. Well, I've taken one other woman abroad in this jet."

Bianca gave him a narrow eye. "Just one?"

He laughed. "What did you think I'd say—thousands?"

"No, I just figured…"

"Well, you figured wrong," he said coolly. "The press loves to embellish a so-called playboy's life and times—it comes with the territory. The truth is, I've always been very particular about who I've involved myself with, especially where it concerns traveling to other countries."

Bianca looked at him thoughtfully. "So she must have been pretty special, then?" Bianca wondered if it was the lady who had barged into his office that one day with a chip on her shoulder.

"Not that special," Tanner responded, sipping his drink.

"So, why were you with her?" she asked.

He paused. "We were having an affair. She was separated from her husband and unhappy."

Bianca cocked a brow with surprise. It wasn't so much that the woman was separated, but that he went after her. Or was it the other way around?

"What happened with her, if I may ask?"

Tanner tasted more of the cocktail. "She broke it off and ended up going back to her husband. Turns out, she wasn't that unhappy, just looking to have a good time on the side. I fell for it, and that was that."

"Were you in love with her?" Bianca had to ask, even if she feared hearing the answer.

"No, it was never about love," he said bluntly. "It was just a physical attraction where one thing led to another."

Bianca felt relieved that he wasn't still pining for another woman. Though that told her nothing about whether or not there was love in his heart for her.

As she pondered this, Bianca was caught off guard when Tanner kissed her.

"What was that for?" she asked.

He grinned. "Do I need a reason to kiss my lady?"

"No, but—"

Tanner put a finger to her lips. "No buts. It doesn't matter who I was with, or who you were with in the past. We're with each other right now. Isn't that what's most important?"

Bianca met his eyes, realizing she was nitpicking things that were beyond her control. They were together as a couple. She had to be grateful for that and let things progress as they were meant to.

She smiled at him. "Yes, that is what's most important."

"Good." He showed his teeth. "So relax and get ready for the time of your life."

"I am ready for it," she declared.

"Are you?"

"Yes." Bianca decided to show him. She held his chin, and this time she initiated the kiss. It started off slow and gradually their mouths opened wide and the kiss became all-consuming, causing her nipples to tingle and other sensations to erupt between her legs.

She wanted to make love to him on the flight, but wasn't sure she was quite that brave. One of the crew members might come back and see them.

Tanner seemed to read her mind as he pulled their lips apart. "It's all right," he said, taking a condom out of a drawer. "We won't be disturbed."

Bianca felt at ease on that score. "Was this part of your master plan...to seduce me in midflight?"

He chuckled lasciviously. "Now just who's seducing whom, here? I want to make love to you every chance I get—whether it's on a plane, in a bedroom or anywhere else. Can you tell me you don't feel the same way?"

She sighed and admitted desirously, "No, I can't."

Tanner used that cue to rip open the condom packet before passionately kissing Bianca again. She reciprocated while eagerly awaiting what would come next.

After the jet landed at Heathrow Airport, they were picked up by a limousine. Tanner smiled at Bianca, his thoughts fresh from their hot sex on his jet. It seemed as though each time they made love was better than the last, making him want her all the more.

He put those fond memories and his libido on hold as he pressed the cell phone to his ear to take a call from Edward Gromley, an important business associate. It was Tanner's hope that the Aloha Seas would become a major tourist destination for Brits traveling to Las Vegas. Indeed, he envisioned all of Europe finding his hotel and casino the place to go when seeking a slice of Hawaii on the mainland, with gambling and first-class entertainment thrown into the bargain.

They checked into a five-star hotel and went up to a penthouse suite complete with designer furnishings and panoramic views of London's skyline.

"It's beautiful," marveled Bianca as they stood by the window.

"So are you," Tanner told her seductively. "It's a perfect combination."

She smiled and kissed him. "You're pretty perfect, yourself."

"Thanks, but I accept the fact that I have a few flaws. Being with you helps me to look past those flaws and bring out my better qualities."

"It's nice to know I can do that," she said humbly.

"For you and me both," he told her, and kissed her lips. Everything she did brightened his existence at every turn.

The next morning, Tanner met with his team of business associates for a meeting in the conference section of the suite. Bianca had used the time to go shopping, expecting to find some gems for her wardrobe. He had insisted on giving her some spending money, having little doubt that anything she purchased would look great on her.

After a few hours of strategizing, Tanner was convinced that a plan was in place to promote the Aloha Seas in London and elsewhere in the United Kingdom, partly by offering some discounted package deals that couldn't be matched by their competitors. He was willing to bite the bullet now in order to gain loyal visitors and expand the reach of the hotel and casino later.

"Thanks for coming," Tanner told Edward and the others present.

"Our pleasure," Edward said with a thick British accent. "I'm sure the Aloha Seas will become a standard for first-rate hotels and casinos in Las Vegas and, indeed, around the world."

"I expect that to be the case," Tanner said. In fact, he already considered the Aloha Seas to represent the finest in hotel ambiance and accommodations, as well as casinos, anywhere.

This trip would only bolster that point on an international stage.

Bianca could barely believe that she was actually walking the streets of London. It was definitely a happening city, and she could see why so many people flocked there as visitors and permanent residents.

She stepped inside Harrods—arguably the world's most famous department store—and was awed by its sheer size. *I would probably need a lot more time than I have to really take it all in,* she thought, while wishing Madison was with her to share this experience.

Maybe one day they could come here together and bring their men along for the ride. Bianca assumed her man would be Tanner, as she couldn't imagine being in London with anyone else.

After purchasing some lingerie and shoes, Bianca

did a bit of shopping at Debenhams and Fenwick before stopping at a place for afternoon tea, where she tried some finger sandwiches, followed by scones with cream and dried fruit.

While there, Bianca called Madison and told her about a few things she bought for her and the twins.

"That's so thoughtful of you! Thank you," Madison said.

"What's a sister and aunt for," Bianca asked, "if not to get some nice gifts from faraway places?"

Madison laughed. "I think you're right."

Bianca smiled while thinking that Madison could soon make her an aunt again. "You really should be here," she told her. "You would love it!"

"I know," Madison agreed. "But it's great that Tanner took you along and that you're turning the visit into a romantic escapade."

"Yes, I'm very happy about that." Bianca sipped her tea thoughtfully. "Who knows what magic we will conjure up after his meetings are finished?"

Madison giggled. "I'm sure you'll be able to think of something."

In her mind, Bianca already had. And it was not only just in the bedroom. She was sure she and Tanner would be on the same page as they tried to make the most out of their time together in London.

"Nice," Tanner said as he watched Bianca hold up the clothing and lingerie she'd bought.

"You think?" she asked.

"Absolutely! I especially can't wait to see you in the lingerie."

Her lashes flickered playfully. "Sure you're not thinking more about me wearing nothing at all?"

"That, too," he admitted. "But still, sexy lingerie will definitely look great on your body."

She beamed. "Well, you'll get your wish later. First, I thought we'd take a cycling tour of the city."

"Oh, really?" Tanner gazed at her.

She nodded. "Seemed like a perfect way to explore London for two fitness buffs."

He grinned, happy to take full advantage of what the city had to offer. "Well, I can hardly argue with that. You're on."

"Great!" Bianca smiled. "Then I thought we'd go dancing at one of those hot Latin clubs here."

"Are you sure you can keep up with me on the dance floor?" Tanner asked.

"I can certainly try," she answered confidently.

"So let's do it." He paused. "Any other tricks up your sleeve?"

Bianca thought about it. "Well, since you asked… On Saturday, I was hoping we could visit the Museum of London. I've always wanted to go there. Then maybe we can check out Trafalgar Square."

Tanner laughed. "You're really into this, aren't you?"

"Yes, culture and history have always interested me," she told him. "It will be great to take back the memories and give me added incentive to visit again."

"We can do whatever you want," he said cheerfully, enjoying the prospect of hanging out as a couple outside of their comfort zone.

She cozied up to him. "Thank you, but it's not just about me. If there's something you want to do—other than you know what, which we both want—let me know and we'll do it."

Tanner grinned. "I'll take that into consideration. In the meantime, I'll settle for this—"

He tilted his face and kissed her passionately.

## Chapter 20

After dancing the night away, Bianca and Tanner went back to the hotel and wasted little time in their desire to have each other, ripping their clothes off and sharing hot kisses in the process.

Bianca envisioned them making love at that moment, and she became wet with lust.

"Do you have protection?" she asked casually.

"Yeah." He dug the packet out of his pants on the floor, handing it to her.

Bianca opened the foil with her teeth and removed the condom, fitting it snugly over his manhood. Then she began kissing his mouth ravenously, slipping her tongue in and out, wanting all of him.

Tanner scooped her into his arms and carried her to the bed, even as their lips remained locked. Only after he laid her down, climbing halfway atop her, did he remove his mouth from hers. He began to sprinkle her face and neck with kisses, causing Bianca's skin to sizzle in their wake. The kisses moved to her breasts, where Tanner generously licked her nipples. It was all she could do not to scream out in ecstasy.

After kissing her stomach, Tanner lowered his face between her legs and flicked his tongue expertly up and down her clitoris. Bianca moaned at the sheer intensity of pleasure that gnawed her nerve endings. Unable to contain herself, she grabbed his head, moving it up and down wildly, so his mouth continued to hit the mark with unrelenting joy. She shuddered violently and heard the cries erupt from her throat as the orgasm reached its peak.

But instead of feeling satisfied, Bianca's need to have Tanner make love to her only grew stronger.

"I'm yours…"

"Damned right, you are," he said, shifting his body up level with hers.

He put her splayed legs over his shoulders and entered her. Bianca winced while adjusting her body to a comfortable position. She arched her back and brought herself halfway to him with every powerful thrust, drunk with the desire of their passionate sex.

Her moans grew louder, and so did his, as Tanner went deep into her in rapid-fire motion. Bianca clamped around his manhood in steadfast contractions, loving the thick feel of him filling her with carnal glee.

Her nipples burned joyously as they rubbed against his rock-hard chest, and their bodies were slick from perspiration and togetherness. Bianca cupped Tanner's cheeks and urged his face to hers. She kissed and nibbled on his lips, tasting remnants of the wine they had enjoyed earlier. She gripped his buttocks as the frenetic pace of their sex rocked the bed.

Soon, their breathing became erratic and their kisses deepened as the moment of impact hit them like a bolt of lightning. While Tanner pounded her, Bianca felt herself levitating with pleasure that was like nothing she had experienced before. She raked her nails across his back and gripped his shoulders with her ankles as their mutual orgasms came in deep waves of delight.

Caught up in their passion, Bianca absorbed Tanner's mighty thrusts, determined to pleasure her man as he pleasured her, squeezing the head of his manhood as it worked its magic on her erogenous zone. He groaned euphorically and his body shuddered in response.

They kissed succulently through the burst of sexual intimacy and as it began to wind down.

When it was over, their limbs slowly untangled and Bianca ended atop Tanner, his arms holding their naked bodies together as though attached. She could hear his heartbeat begin to return to normal while her own continued to pound. She breathed in the scent of their sex, stimulating to Bianca and effective in binding her to her lover.

In that moment, she realized with unmistakable clarity what she could no longer deny. She had fallen in love with Tanner Long.

It was something she wanted to share with him, and she expected to hear the same in return, if his actions were any indication.

"I love you," she said softly.

Bianca heard the words again in her head as she waited for Tanner to respond. At first, she wondered if he'd heard her clearly. Then she feared that he had, but was unable to give his love back.

After a moment or two of regret, Bianca heard Tanner's slow but steady breathing and had her answer, though not the one she wanted.

He had fallen asleep and hadn't heard her declaration of love.


A week later, Tanner stepped into Solomon's office and did a double take. His brother, who was talking on the phone, had shaved his head bald. This was definitely something that would take Tanner a while to get used to. Unlike him, Solomon had always had some hair on his head.

Tanner took a seat and waited for Solomon to end the conversation. His thoughts turned to Bianca. He was still riding high from the trip to England. Once the business part of the trip was done, they had spent the rest of the time having fun in and out of bed. The experience was so satisfying that he would gladly go across the pond again with her.

Hell, he would go anywhere with Bianca, whom Tanner was beginning to feel was meant to be a major part of his life, much as his brother was… Only, as a romantic mate that he could grow with over time.

Tanner thought he may have even heard Bianca say she loved him when they were in London, just after they made scrumptious love. But since he had fallen asleep almost immediately after their hot, energy-draining sex, he figured it must have been a dream.

*I don't want to jump the gun and make false assumptions,* he told himself. Nor was he keen on confessing his own love for the gorgeous woman until he was absolutely certain that he was the man she wanted to spend the rest of her life with.

Was that asking too much? Tanner wondered. Or not

asking enough for someone who could potentially become his wife and the mother of his children?

When Solomon got off the phone, Tanner wasted little time in asking, "Where the hell did your hair go?"

Solomon smiled, running a hand across the top of his smooth head. "Got rid of it."

"Why?"

He shrugged. "Just wanted to try a new look. Figured I'd follow your lead, while keeping my head from feeling so hot when I'm outside at this time of the year."

Tanner smiled. "I'm happy to be a role model for you, but it takes work to stay bald when it's not natural."

"My barber will take care of that," Solomon argued confidently. "Besides, being bald seems to have served you well enough."

"It has," admitted Tanner. "But, then again, I have been bald for a long time and for myself, not others."

"Same here," Solomon insisted. "That said, some women have told me they find bald men sexier. Maybe now I'm listening to them."

"It doesn't seem like you've had too much trouble with women finding you sexy up to this point."

"True enough." Solomon leaned forward. "Still, it's time for a change. I think I feel sexier and more professional in my appearance."

Tanner laughed. "Guess it's all a state of mind. If it works for you, then welcome to the bald club."

Solomon chuckled and they turned their attention back to the business of profitably running Aloha Seas.

Tanner made the rounds at the hotel-casino, greeting guests warmly. He wanted the Aloha Seas to be a welcoming environment for all. Besides the adult activities, there was plenty to keep children occupied as well, such as swimming, games, exhibits, shopping and, of course, eating. The way he saw it, the place was meant to be a tropical playground with something for everyone, ensuring a continual source of guests, with many already locked in for return visits.

*I couldn't be happier being a force to be reckoned with in Vegas,* Tanner thought, even if that didn't necessarily define him. But it was his vision as a businessman, and so far the success was undeniable.

What he hadn't expected was to be so happy right now in his personal life. Bianca had come into his life at just the right time, giving him the type of romantic stability and intellectual companionship he needed. Plus the passions generated when they were intimate left him both exhilarated and wanting more at every opportunity.

This confirmed to him that she was a lady he never wanted to get out of his system. And, if he had his way, he never would.

Tanner stepped into the spacious outdoor area where they had a nightly luau, bringing a Hawaiian tradition straight to Las Vegas with native cuisine, including a kalua pig cooked in an imu, fish imported from the islands, Hawaiian sweet potatoes and Mai Tais.

He spotted Bianca, who was waiting for him so they could feast and take in the show together. It was the second time they had attended the Aloha Seas luau, and Tanner looked forward to it even more now, as their relationship had progressed to the point that they were practically like an old, but still sexy, married couple.

"Aloha!" he said to her, grinning.

"Aloha," she said, flashing her teeth. "Thought I might have to do this one alone."

"Not a chance." Tanner kissed her. "We've added a bit to the entertainment that I can't wait to see."

"More gorgeous hula dancers?" Bianca teased him.

He eyed her sweetly. "Not more gorgeous than you."

"I don't know about that," she said.

"I do," he insisted. "Maybe you should try your hand at hula dancing. I'll bet you'd be damned good swaying those hips."

She laughed. "Maybe I'll give you a private show one of these days."

He liked the idea of that, envisioning it. "Ready whenever you are."

"I'm sure you are," she said attractively.

They then took their seats and enjoyed some Hawaiian music before eating. Tanner had fun feeding Bianca with his hands and, in turn, being fed by her. It was indicative of the comfort level their relationship had attained. He imagined it would only get better over time.

Tanner had his arm around Bianca, and she leaned her head on his shoulder as they listened to Hawaiians tell stories about their ancestors and the fascinating history of the islands.

Then female and male hula dancers took to the stage and shook their hips to traditional and contemporary Polynesian music and drumbeats. Then fire knife dancers wowed the audience with heart-pounding, daring routines that left the audience gasping.

When it was over, Tanner knew that Bianca had been thoroughly engrossed by the luau. He felt the same way and thought that Hawaii should be the next big trip they made together to explore the islands and each other in possibly the best romantic setting in the world.

After the show, Tanner led Bianca up to his suite to take an already splendid evening to the next level.

## Chapter 21

In late August, Bianca was two weeks late for her period. But she wasn't sure she should be worried quite yet. She and Tanner had always used protection during intercourse, so she couldn't be pregnant, could she?

Though she did want to become a mother someday, she was not in favor of having a child out of wedlock. Knowing how hard it was for single mothers trying to raise children, it wouldn't be fair to her or the child.

And how would Tanner feel about becoming a father? Would he somehow blame her? Or accuse her of trying to trap him?

Would it be a big imposition on his comfortable lifestyle as the unmarried CEO of a hotel and casino to also have to be a daddy?

Bianca recalled that she told Tanner she loved him in London. He had apparently not heard her and never responded. But did that mean he didn't feel the same way?

She'd lost her nerve and never brought it up again.

*Maybe I should have,* she thought, sitting at an outdoor café while waiting for Melanie.

But she hadn't been eager to pour her heart out only to be told it was one-sided, even if they were totally compatible sexually.

Bianca sucked in a deep breath over her bottle of fruit juice, realizing she was probably worrying over nothing. Many women miss periods for one reason or another other than pregnancy.

Bianca took solace in that thought as she greeted Melanie.

"Sorry I'm late," she said. "Ivan dropped by."

Ivan was a local television personality Melanie was dating.

"No problem," Bianca told her honestly.

After ordering, Melanie regarded Bianca curiously. "So what's going on? By your tone, I got the impression you were worried about something."

Having already opened the door to this conversation, Bianca told her about her missed period, hoping Melanie would dismiss it as nothing to be alarmed about at the moment. Especially since they had used condoms every time.

"It could be for any number of reasons," Melanie remarked. "A friend of mine had the same thing happen and it ended up being because she was under a lot of stress. I've heard that some women are late because of weight gain or loss, changes in lifestyle, travel, you name it."

"I've read about that, too," Bianca told her.

"Still, you should take a pregnancy test, if only for peace of mind."

Bianca frowned. "I was afraid you'd say that."

"Hey, I'm just being real," Melanie said. "Accidents

do happen, even with condoms. The test is quick and easy. If it's negative, it puts your mind at ease. If not, then you—and Tanner—will have to deal with it."

"Not sure he's ready to do that," Bianca muttered bleakly. "Not sure I am."

"Listen, you like the man a lot, and from everything you've told me he's just as taken with you. So maybe Tanner's not the jerk his brother is. If that's the case, he'll do the right thing by you if you're carrying his baby."

Bianca drank her juice thoughtfully. What was the right thing? Did she really want to bring a child into this world without having the love of the child's father?

Or was she just worrying needlessly when there was a good chance she wasn't even pregnant? If she wasn't, Tanner would be off the hook as a daddy.

The following morning, Bianca took the test. Her heart pounded and all types of thoughts rolled through her head. Would the result be a blessing or a curse? Would Tanner feel the same way?

It took only a minute, then she watched the results unfold before her eyes as the colored bands appeared.

Bianca gasped as the full realization hit her. She was pregnant with Tanner's baby.

*How will he handle this news?* she asked herself uneasily. How should she handle it?

What if he rejected his own child? Could she actually go it alone as a single mom? Or was that too much when she had enough on her plate as an entertainment reporter and a CEO's girlfriend?

*I have to tell Tanner,* a voice within stated nervously. Then deal with it.

Bianca dialed his number, then immediately disconnected, believing this was something she needed to do in person. She owed them both that much, given the implications that her being pregnant carried for both of them.

Bianca grabbed her purse and headed out the door.

Once inside the Aloha Seas, she called Tanner, realizing that with his busy schedule he could be anywhere.

He answered right away. "Hey," he said in his usual pleasant tone.

"Hi." Bianca tried to keep her voice from shaking. "Where are you?"

"At work." Tanner paused. "Where are you?"

"I'm at the hotel," she said. "I need to see you—"

"Is everything okay?" he asked, the slightest concern in his voice.

"I'm fine." She sighed. "Can we meet at your suite?"

"Sure. Give me five minutes."

"See you then."

Bianca disconnected. *Now comes the hard part,* she thought, heading for the elevator.

Tanner cut his meeting short. There had been a sense of urgency in Bianca's voice. Or was that just his imagination? Probably, he told himself, considering she said she was fine. Yet, there was obviously something on her mind. He hoped she wasn't coming to tell him that their romance had come to an end and she was moving on. That would devastate him to no end, as he saw nothing but a bright future for them.

*I won't jump to the wrong conclusions,* he thought. Could be that she was in the mood to have sex and couldn't wait. That idea turned him on.

He found Bianca waiting outside his door when he

got up to the penthouse. As always, she was a sight for sore eyes.

"Hey," he said.

"Hey." She smiled slightly.

"Came as soon as I could."

"Thanks," she said.

He unlocked the door and they went inside.

Studying her, Tanner thought he detected a slight quiver of Bianca's lower lip. "Are you sure nothing's wrong?" he asked, meeting her eyes.

"I'm pregnant," she blurted out.

His eyes widened in shock. "Are you sure?"

"I took a pregnancy test. It was positive."

Tanner drew in breath while trying to understand this. "But how? We used condoms every time."

"Condoms can break," she responded tersely. "That must have been the case here."

He had heard that, but never experienced it before, that he knew of. "Wow…" he said tonelessly.

"That's what I thought, too." Bianca paused. "Just thought you should know…"

Tanner briefly considered that maybe it wasn't his child. But the thought was only fleeting, as he knew she wasn't the type of woman to sleep around. This was something they both shared responsibility for.

"What do you want to do about it?" he asked straightforwardly.

Her lashes fluttered. "If you're asking if I plan to have an abortion, the answer is no."

"I wasn't." He had hoped she would say what he was thinking. That left him to do so. Taking her hand, Tanner looked at Bianca squarely and said, "We have to get married."

Her head snapped back. "What?"

"I want to marry you, Bianca," Tanner repeated. "We're having a baby. I don't want the child born out of wedlock. It's the right thing to do."

"I'm not going to marry you because *it's the right thing to do*," she said, removing her hand from his. "People have babies all the time without being married. It's not the end of the world."

"That may be, but those weren't *my* children," he declared. "Our child deserves the best we can provide him or her—starting with a stable home."

Bianca's brows touched. "Are you saying I can't provide a stable home?"

He scratched his nose thoughtfully. "No, of course not. What I'm saying is that a child coming into this world should be in a home with two loving parents. If we marry, we can provide that for our child—under one roof. Or if you prefer that we just live together—"

"I don't prefer either," she said irritably. "I don't want to marry you or live together simply for the sake of our child. I haven't heard anything from your mouth about being in love with me. Without love, what's the point of living under the same roof, married or not?"

Tanner understood where she was coming from. Although he had not heard the words come from her mouth, either. Did that mean she wasn't as keen on him as he thought?

"I think we know how we feel about each other," he told her.

"I'm not sure we do," she countered.

He sighed. "Of course I love you."

"Do you really?" She had a hand on her hip.

"Yeah, I do," he confessed. He didn't need the words back to know marrying her was the right move, especially considering that she was now carrying his child.

Bianca wrinkled her nose. "And it took me getting pregnant to force the words out of you?"

Tanner raised a brow, not expecting to be given the third degree. "We've both spoken with our hearts and bodies," he said unevenly.

"I spoke the words out loud," she told him thoughtfully, "but you'd fallen asleep, so…"

"Why didn't you wake me?"

She considered this. "Just didn't feel right."

He flashed a steady gaze. "Well, I'm awake now and hopefully neither of our feelings has changed any…"

Bianca met his eyes. "I'm not sure what to believe or what to say—other than that I cannot marry you when it seems like you are more interested in doing the honorable thing for your child than truly wanting me as your wife."

"You've got it all wrong," he insisted.

"I don't think so." She spoke flatly. "If you had really wanted to marry me, you would have asked me before now. But that wasn't the case, was it?"

Tanner stood there, speechless, even though he knew that not asking her before now had less to do with him than her. He'd needed to know how she felt about him and a future together as much as she wanted to hear his feelings before he declared his love and popped the question.

"Right. I didn't think so." Bianca narrowed her eyes. "Goodbye, Tanner."

"Don't we need to talk about this some more?"

"There's really nothing more to talk about," she responded. "I came here to say what I had to. I don't intend to keep you out of your child's life, but I need some time to think. I hope you can respect that."

He sucked in a deep breath, choosing not to argue

with her in what seemed to be a losing proposition. "Yeah, sure," he uttered. "Do what you need to do."

"Thank you," she said meekly and left.

Tanner wanted, with everything he had, to go after her. But doing so would only drive her further away. What should have been one of the happiest days of their lives had turned out to be anything but. And, at least for the moment, there wasn't a damned thing he could do about it, other than try to figure out a way to win her back so they and their child could live together as a family.

## Chapter 22

Later, curled up on her couch, Bianca wasn't sure she'd handled telling Tanner about the pregnancy in the right way. She honestly had not expected him to ask her to marry him after she revealed she was pregnant. On the contrary, she had feared that he might blow a gasket in having to deal with being a father in his well-structured life. Under other circumstances, she would have jumped at the chance to become Mrs. Tanner Long. What woman wouldn't want that with all he had to offer a wife?

But as an independent woman who didn't need someone to take care of her as an obligation, she couldn't have lived with herself had she agreed to marry him for all the wrong reasons. In her mind, being a dad was not enough of a reason, in and of itself. After all, nowadays a woman didn't need to be wed to a man simply because he had impregnated her. Unless they were more concerned about financial security than love.

*I'd much rather know that a man was in love with me, wanting us to live together as man and wife—not being there to micromanage the mother of his child,* Bianca told herself.

Yes, the sex between them was incredible and the chemistry undeniable. But she'd always viewed those as stepping stones to a lifelong commitment rather than taking the place of it.

She was happy that Tanner seemed genuine in his desire to become a dad, knowing that many men would have shirked their responsibility. *I love the thought of him being the father of my child,* she mused.

That didn't mean, though, that they belonged together in matrimony.

After making herself a cup of raspberry leaf tea, Bianca phoned Madison for a video chat, needing to talk to someone other than Tanner.

"Well, hello," her sister chirped.

"Hello… Do you have time to talk?"

"I can find the time."

"I won't take too long," Bianca promised. She was mindful that Madison had two kids and a husband to take care of. *How will I manage with one child on my own?* she asked herself.

"Uh-oh…something's wrong," Madison surmised.

Bianca raised her brow. "Am I that transparent?"

"Yes, I'm afraid so. Tell me—"

Bianca paused. "I'm pregnant."

Madison put a hand to her mouth. "You're not."

"I am." Bianca licked her lips. "And no, it wasn't planned." She felt a little guilty that she got pregnant by accident when Madison was actually trying to conceive, thus far with no luck. How was that right?

"So do I congratulate you or...?" Madison asked with a straight face.

Bianca sighed. "Probably the 'or' would be better."

"I see." Madison was thoughtful. "Does Tanner know?"

"Yes."

"And..."

Bianca took a moment before saying, "He asked me to marry him."

"That's bad news?" asked Madison.

"I didn't say that."

Madison frowned. "So why do I sense you're not happy to marry a man you're crazy about?"

Bianca tasted the coffee and responded miserably, "He never said he loved me or wanted to marry me until I told him I was pregnant."

"Maybe that was what he needed to step up to the plate," Madison suggested.

"But it's not what I need in a husband," Bianca told her frankly.

"I disagree. I think Tanner is exactly what you need in a husband and the father of the child you're carrying. Don't let pride stand in the way of being with the man of your dreams."

"That's just it," Bianca offered. "I'm not sure if I'm the woman of Tanner's dreams. Do I really need to be with a man who seems to only want to make it legal for the child?"

"Is that really so bad?" questioned Madison, fluttering her lashes. "Tanner's loaded and wants to do right by you and your unborn child. Why not let him do it? We both know you've dated a few jerks and got nothing for your trouble but bad memories. With Tanner, you're getting someone solid, more than capable of giving you and your child a good life and he definitely cares for you. In my book, that's not a person you give up on."

Bianca reflected on Madison's words of wisdom and found the logic hard to ignore. She and Tanner were good together. Even if what he felt for her was something less than pure love, she was certain he would be a great father and a good person to have as her husband.

*And if he doesn't truly love me, it doesn't mean he couldn't grow into it eventually,* she told herself.

"So, what are you thinking?" Madison asked. "I assume it's not to mind my own business. After all, you called me, remember?"

Bianca smiled. "Yes, I did and I welcome your input into my somewhat delicate situation. You know, you're right. Why should I reject outright Tanner's wish to marry me before our baby is born? I do love him. Maybe that will be enough, given the other ways in which we click."

"Maybe it will be," Madison agreed. "Besides, I want my big sister to join me in matrimony, giving us another reason to visit each other."

"That would be nice, to get together as wives," Bianca said, knowing it would take time to adjust to being a wife.

"And mothers," Bianca reminded her.

"Right." Bianca chuckled softly and then thought about Madison's attempts to get pregnant. "I'm sorry it's me and not you having a baby."

"Don't be. I already have two. Besides, we're still trying to add to our family and my doctor tells me there's no reason why we shouldn't. It'll happen when it's time. And he or she will have an older cousin to look up to."

Bianca smiled. "True enough."

"Well, I hope everything between you and Tanner gets back on track."

"I hope so, too," Bianca said optimistically. "I'll let you know where things stand later."

"Please do," Madison told her. "It would be wonderful to head back to Vegas for a wedding. I can also help you with the planning, sending out invitations, whatever."

"I appreciate that and I'll take you up on it, I'm sure." But first she had to make things right with Tanner, knowing they had parted on a sour note.

Tanner met Solomon in the Island Lounge, still trying to come to terms with the news Bianca had just laid on him. And even more, with her rejection of his love and marriage proposal.

"So, what's up?" Solomon asked, sitting at the table. "If this is about the budget and—"

"It isn't," Tanner said concisely, knowing that the financial health of the hotel-casino was solid in his brother's more-than-capable hands. "It's personal."

Solomon raised a brow. "You're not sick, are you?"

"Not physically."

"Did you and Bianca have a fight or something?" Solomon asked.

Tanner paused, nursing his drink. "Bianca's pregnant."

"Wow." Solomon lifted the beer Tanner had ordered for him. "How did that happen?"

"It was an accident," Tanner said simply.

Solomon regarded him. "You sure about that?"

Tanner met his gaze. "What are you saying?"

"Only that having your baby is a way to keep a hand

in your pocket, whether the relationship survives or not."

"Bianca wouldn't do that." Tanner defended her, knowing it had nothing to do with money. "Besides, we used condoms every time."

"Look, I'm not saying she was trying to trap you or anything, but it is what it is," Solomon said. "You're going to be a daddy and child support can add up over time."

"I don't give a damn about that," Tanner spoke bluntly. "I have more than enough money to make sure my child has a good life—and Bianca, too."

Solomon sat back. "If you feel that way, why are you down?"

Tanner took a breath. "I asked Bianca to marry me."

"She turned you down?" Solomon looked at him.

"Yeah, she did," Tanner responded glumly.

"Why the hell would she do that?" Solomon asked in disbelief.

"She thinks I only asked her because it was the right thing for the child."

Solomon leaned forward. "Is it true?"

Tanner considered the question, asking himself the same thing. He knew the answer, and had from the moment Bianca gave him the news. Looking directly at Solomon, he replied, "I'm in love with Bianca. In an ideal world, I would have asked her to marry me at some point in the foreseeable future, and then we would have started a family. Once she told me about the pregnancy, it seemed the perfect way to have it all right now."

"But she didn't see it that way?" Solomon asked.

"Guess she expected the whole 'getting on one knee' thing, a ring and my telling her over and over how much I love her," muttered Tanner over his glass of beer. "I just acted the best way I knew how under the circumstances."

"And no one can fault you for that—I certainly can't." Solomon rubbed his chin. "Neither should she."

"So, what should I do?" Tanner asked, not wanting to see their relationship go down the drain. But he didn't want to press her into doing something she didn't want to do.

"I'm probably the last person to give advice on getting someone to marry you," Solomon told him honestly. "I've never gone down that road before. However, I think you need to reassess just how much she cares for you, rather than the other way around—and let that be your guide."

"She says she loves me," Tanner said, even if this had apparently come when he was asleep and not the actual words face-to-face.

"But not enough to marry you?" Solomon rolled his eyes. "I don't get it."

"Yeah, I know how you feel." Tanner sipped his drink. "Women can be complicated."

"Tell me about it. That's probably why I've never gotten close to going down the aisle. Some hassles you just don't need."

"Other women you can't do without," Tanner muttered dryly.

"Just talk to her and see if you can work things out," Solomon suggested. "If not, don't beat yourself up about it. There are other Biancas out there who would not hesitate to be your lady, marriage or not."

"None of them would be *this* Bianca, though," Tanner said, finding it hard to imagine settling for someone else when she was the best woman for him.

"That's not necessarily a bad thing. This will be up

to you to decide, at the end of the day." Solomon paused. "Oh, and whatever happens between you and Bianca, you're still going to be a father and you should be in on any decisions about the child's life."

"I hear you," Tanner murmured thoughtfully. He felt better after having a talk with his brother, in spite of the fact that as a confirmed bachelor, still playing the field, Solomon's mind was on anything but commitment, marriage and children.

*I'm at a different place in my life,* Tanner mused, *thanks to Bianca.* He wanted things to work out with her. Even if they didn't get married, he still wanted to keep seeing her and to be there every step of the way as she went through the pregnancy.

Would she give him that opportunity?

Or would she decide to go it alone and pierce his heart in the process?

## Chapter 23

Bianca stepped into the Aloha Seas, wishing she could turn back the clock a day. Or maybe even longer, to when she had unknowingly gotten pregnant. But she couldn't change the past. Instead, she could only deal with the present and future, and any adjustments along the way.

The fact was, she loved Tanner and could not turn her back on that or him. Whether he had told her the same beforehand or not, she had to take a leap of faith that the father of her unborn child was the man she belonged with in matrimony. Whatever issues they needed to work out along the way, she was confident they could and would.

"Hello."

She turned to see Frank.

"Hi," Bianca responded.

"Let me guess...you're looking for Tanner, right?"

She smiled, wondering if Tanner had made him privy to their situation. "Yes, I thought I'd surprise him and take him out to lunch, if he's not too busy."

"In fact, our meeting just broke up, so I'm sure he has time to go to lunch with his lady."

Bianca glowed, appreciating the term *lady*. "Great," she said.

"The last I saw, he was still in our conference room. I can give him a call and—"

"That's okay," she said. "I know the way." Tanner had given her a tour of the conference room and his office early on.

"No problem." Frank grinned. "Enjoy your lunch."

"I will."

Bianca made her way through the hotel while wondering how she could have freaked out about Tanner asking him to marry her. Perhaps the pregnancy and proposal had all just happened too fast. She'd never doubted that Tanner's heart was in the right place, even if he hadn't come out with the words "I love you" until almost pressed into them.

*I was basically guilty of the same thing,* she told herself, considering he had been asleep when she confessed her feelings to him.

She was sure they could talk things through, deal with their pregnancy together and make their romance official.

After rounding a corner in a long hallway, Bianca approached a conference room where she heard muffled voices. One of the double doors was partially ajar.

She peeked in and immediately honed in on the back of Tanner's bald head. He stood near the center of the room. Her eyes widened with shock as Bianca realized he was kissing Kendre Kelly. And vice versa. Their arms were wrapped tightly around each other as if they were lovers.

Bianca's jaw dropped. She wondered if she were somehow having a nightmare.

As much as she wished that had been the case, it was clear to her that what she was witnessing was anything but her imagination.

She'd caught the man of her dreams, love of her life and father of her unborn child in a French kiss with his singing sensation.

*You bastard,* Bianca cursed within.

In that instant, Kendre opened her eyes and seemed to look right at Bianca gleefully while continuing to stick her tongue down Tanner's throat and rub her hands over his head with no resistance whatsoever from him.

Having had enough, Bianca backed away from the door, deciding not to make a scene. Obviously, Tanner had already chosen to move in a new direction. Or had he and Kendre been romantically involved all the time he had been dating Bianca?

Suppressing tears, she couldn't get out of the hotel-casino soon enough. She couldn't begin to express how betrayed she felt. How could Tanner do such a thing? Was casual sex with Kendre worth losing what Bianca believed was a real relationship?

She nearly ran into Frank.

"Did you find him?" he asked casually.

Bianca hardly knew what to say. Or what not to. "He was already gone," she lied.

"Sorry about that."

No sorrier than she was at that moment. "It's all right. I'll call him."

Frank favored her with a disappointed look, having no idea of what she had caught Tanner doing.

"I'm sure Tanner will make it up to you," he said.

*I don't see how he ever could,* Bianca thought sadly. "I have to go."

"Bye," Frank offered kindly.

"Bye," Bianca managed to get out and walked away before she ran into Tanner and Kendre, who would no doubt only give some lame excuses were she to call them out on what she saw.

She didn't care to listen, as she had seen the proof with her own eyes. And with it went any chance of a happily ever after for her and Tanner.

"Can't say I didn't warn you," Melanie said the next day as she sat beside Bianca on her porch. "He's such a sleaze, just like his brother."

"Yeah, tell me about it." Bianca stewed. She hated that Melanie was right, after all, in her belief that Tanner and Solomon cared a lot more about themselves than anyone else.

"I can't believe he asked you to marry him and make a proper home for his baby and the next day he's making out with Kendre Kelly," Melanie voiced tartly over her glass of wine. "Then again, I totally *can* believe it. That's what powerful, good-looking men do—they reel you in and then cut you loose when things get too hot."

"But why Kendre?" Bianca couldn't help but ask. "I knew she wanted Tanner, but he denied any interest in her. Was he two-timing me from the start?" *Could he have been that much of a jerk while making me believe otherwise?* she wondered.

"Who knows?" Melanie rolled her eyes. "I wouldn't be surprised at all. I've read that Kendre Kelly has a power over men, and she can get just about anyone she sets her sights on to drop everything to have sex with her."

"Why couldn't she go after someone else, then?" Bianca asked angrily.

"Because that's how many women are—especially spoiled, rich ones who think they're entitled."

*"Damn her,"* spat Bianca and sipped water from a bottle, feeling sorry for herself.

"Damn *him!"* Melanie retorted and tasted wine. "Why do we always blame the women, and not the men who cheat on us?"

"I definitely blame him for what I saw," Bianca snapped. "There's nothing he can say to justify locking lips with Kendre."

"I agree. And chances are that wasn't the first time they hooked up—and it more than likely has gone well beyond kissing, if you know what I mean."

Bianca knew all too well. She hated the idea of her man being intimate with another woman—or maybe even more than one. Especially when she thought he was perfectly content with their sexual connection.

How could she have been so blind?

"Maybe, when I said I wouldn't marry him, he just lost it—" Bianca suggested.

"Yeah, right—and Kendre was there to help him find his way?" Melanie said. "I don't think so. If Tanner cared for you at all, he wouldn't have jumped another woman's bones the next day rather than trying to work things out with you."

"I suppose you're right," Bianca said, unable to make sense of it.

"No suppose about it! I am right. Don't go blaming yourself for something that clearly wasn't your fault. Rather than step up like a man and fight for you, Tan-

ner caved in and allowed himself to fall victim to Kendre's advances. If you ask me, he's a sorry excuse for
a human being."

"He's certainly not the man I thought he was." Bianca
was willing to concede that, if nothing else.

"Most men aren't," Melanie said. "That's why it's
so hard for us to find anyone worthy of our affections."

Bianca sat back pensively. "I'm still pregnant with
Tanner's child. How do I deal with that?" The thought
of raising the child all by herself scared her. But did
she even want Tanner to be in the child's life, always
reminding her of his betrayal?

"You deal with it the same way women have dealt
with it for centuries," Melanie responded flatly. "You
get what you can in child support—which in this case,
should be plenty—and raise the child the best you can."

"I'm sure Tanner will want to be a part of the baby's
life," Bianca said. At least that was the vibe she picked
up from him after he'd learned she was pregnant as
well as in previous discussions about the importance
of family.

"So, let him," Melanie told her. "That's the least he
can do. But that doesn't mean Tanner has to be a part
of your life. He gave up that right when he turned to
Kendre Kelly."

"I agree," Bianca said painfully, wondering how
things with her and Tanner could have fallen apart so
quickly. Did she ever really know him? Or had one of
the city's most eligible bachelors merely been playing
her all along, insincere about everything he said he
stood for?

# Chapter 24

Tanner hadn't spoken to Bianca in over a week. It wasn't from lack of trying. After he'd heard that she had come by the hotel-casino to see him before mysteriously leaving without so much as a text, he had left her countless messages on her cell phone, but with no response.

Frankly, he couldn't understand why she was shutting him out. If she didn't want to marry him, that was her choice. But that was no reason why they couldn't at least be civil, especially since she was carrying his baby and he had every intention of being there for him or her. And for Bianca, at least through the pregnancy. Unless that was asking too much of her, too.

He had considered showing up at her house or workplace, but he wouldn't go where he wasn't wanted.

Tanner was in the back of his limousine when he tried Bianca's number again. *Pick up,* he urged silently. *Talk to me.*

What the hell was her problem, anyway? Was she really that pissed that he hadn't told her he loved her and wanted to marry her before she revealed she was pregnant?

It didn't make sense to just throw away everything they had built. Even if they simply continued dating, it would at least still keep them connected as a couple as their child developed before coming into this world.

The limo stopped and Tanner watched as Chuck got inside.

"Hey," his friend and attorney said warmly.

"Hi," Tanner told him as the limo started moving. "Thanks for meeting with me."

"No problem. I had an opening in the schedule. So what's up?"

Tanner barely knew where to begin. Or end, for that matter. But he needed someone to talk to about this outside of Solomon, who was not exactly impartial when it came to seeking advice.

"I'm going to be a father," Tanner said evenly.

"Really?" Chuck lifted a brow. "I guess congratulations are in order, right?"

"Yes and no," Tanner responded as he pondered the question and then told Chuck where things stood with Bianca.

"So let me get this straight," Chuck began. "Bianca tells you she's pregnant, you tell her you love her and want to get married, and she blows you off—"

"More or less," Tanner said disappointedly.

"She still wants you, man—and needs to feel you truly want her."

"But I thought I'd made that perfectly clear." Tanner rolled his eyes.

"Not quite." Chuck gazed at him. "Here's what you need to do, from someone who's been there and also knows a thing or two about give and take." He sighed. "You need to propose properly with a nice ring, down on one knee, professing your love, flowers—the whole nine yards."

Tanner chuckled. "You really believe that would make a difference?"

"Like, a night and day difference," Chuck insisted. "It's what a woman needs from a man—I know Deloris made me do it before she said yes. Try it, and tell Bianca you want her and your child as one unit under one roof after whatever type wedding she wants. That should do the trick."

"And if it doesn't?" Tanner had to ask.

"Then it will be on her and not you. But don't even go there. In this town, you have to believe you will win the game, so to speak. To think otherwise is a recipe for failure."

"Got it." Tanner grinned. "I'll work on that."

Chuck smiled. "Now there's the guy I've come to know."

"I hope so," Tanner said thoughtfully and told Johan to stop the car. "Appreciate your advice."

"Happy to give it," Chuck said. "Just be sure to save me a front-row seat at the wedding."

Tanner smiled, not quite ready yet to make such plans. "When it happens, you can count on it."

He let Chuck out, then asked Johan, "You wouldn't happen to know a good jeweler, would you?"

Looking in the rearview mirror, the driver responded, "Yeah, I think I can help you out there."

Tanner grinned and immediately began to work on a plan to try to win Bianca's heart, just as she had won his.

* * *

Bianca spent the morning doing a story on Cirque du Soleil, interviewing several local performers and how they got involved in the company's amazing entertainment. She wrote her piece and took the rest of the afternoon off. Since the temperature was cooler than usual at this time of year, she went for a brisk walk.

In spite of her attempt to focus on work, exercise or anything else but Tanner, inevitably Bianca found herself coming back to him. She loved that man to death and was carrying his child. Yet none of that seemed to matter—at least not to him—since he had so easily turned his attention to Kendre Kelly.

*I can't compete with her,* Bianca thought. And why should she? No man was worth selling her soul and ignoring her principles. And for what? Giving her love to someone who had thrown it away the first chance he got?

Since Tanner obviously wasn't the man she hoped he would be, Bianca felt she had no choice but to distance herself from him, painful as it was. Though the thought of going it alone with a child scared her, it would be worse to marry or live with a man who obviously didn't truly love her.

Giving up the child was not an option, Bianca knew. No one else could possibly love her child the way she could. If Tanner wanted to be a part of his or her life, as Bianca suspected, he was welcome to. They could work out arrangements for child support and visitation. Other than that, she would live her life and he would live his.

It was too soon for Bianca to even think about someone else taking Tanner's place in her heart. She only wished the same were true for him.

After walking a little longer than usual and feeling

it in her legs, Bianca began to slow down as she neared her house.

Her heart did a little leap when she spotted the familiar limousine out front.

Bianca had a mind to turn around and run away, but knew she would have to confront Tanner sooner or later. *May as well get this over with now,* she told herself.

Even that didn't stop her from shaking like a leaf as the prospect of coming face-to-face with the man she had fallen in love with. Before he ripped her heart out.

Tanner stepped out of the limousine with a bouquet of roses.

"Hey," he said.

She stood, mute, in jogging attire with her hair in a ponytail.

Tanner flashed a genuine smile. "These are for you." He held out the roses.

She looked at them and him, frowning with disapproval. "I don't want them."

His brow furrowed. "What's the matter with you?"

"I think you know."

"I know you turned down my marriage proposal after telling me you were pregnant. I may not have handled it the way you expected me to, but my heart was, and still is, in the right place."

Bianca curled her lip. "Just go."

"Are you really ready to throw away what we had because I never said I loved you before your news?" He gazed at her. "Since I never heard the words from your lips, even if you say you told me, I'd say we're even. That hardly means we should end what we started."

"You ended it when you decided to put your tongue down another woman's throat," she snapped.

Tanner's eyes narrowed. "What the hell are you talking about?"

"Don't play dumb—it doesn't suit you."

Tanner was honestly at a loss and she didn't seem to get that. "Why don't you just spit it out then?"

Bianca sighed. "I came to see you at the hotel, and I saw you in a lip lock with Kendre Kelly."

"What?" Tanner's mouth hung open.

"You heard me."

"That's crazy!" he said, an edge to his tone.

"I know what I saw," Bianca told him. "And it was definitely you. She had her hands all over your bald head."

"It wasn't me," he insisted. "Look, why don't we just go inside and talk about this—"

"I'd rather not. I'm done talking. I don't need someone in my life I can't trust."

Tanner tried to reason with her. "You can trust me."

"I thought I could, but I was obviously mistaken." Bianca sucked in a deep breath. "Other than getting together sometime to talk about what role you want to play in the life of our baby, we're done."

"Just like that?" he asked in disbelief.

"Yes. It's the best thing for me." She looked down and back at him. "I have to go. Please respect my wishes and leave me alone."

Tanner was speechless as she walked away from him for the second time—for all the wrong reasons.

He started to go after her, ignoring Bianca's request. But after taking several steps toward her front door, Tanner stopped his movement, deciding she was in no mood to talk and straighten things out. Maybe he should quit while he was ahead, before making the situation even worse.

Though he wondered if it had already reached the point where there was no turning back. And no moving forward in the future he coveted with Bianca.

# Chapter 25

Tanner walked back and forth in his suite, stunned at the turn of events. Instead of her accepting the roses, which should have been followed by a proposal of marriage, she had rejected his attempt to make things right by accusing him of making out with Kendre Kelly.

As far as he knew, Kendre played the field with any number of men. And he certainly wasn't the only bald-headed guy in town.

That thought prompted another in Tanner's head. Solomon was bald now, too. Could Bianca have mistaken his brother for him?

Was Solomon involved with Kendre Kelly?

Tanner grabbed his keys and left the room after learning Solomon was in the Mahalo Lounge.

There he found his brother at the bar, alone.

"Are you expecting someone?" Tanner asked, sitting beside him.

"No, it's just me." Solomon regarded him. "Do you want to talk about something?"

Tanner met his eyes. "Are you dating Kendre Kelly?"

"No, we're definitely not dating." Solomon cracked a half grin. "At least, I wouldn't call fooling around between consenting adults *dating*."

"So you were kissing her the other day in the hotel?"

"Not in public—it wouldn't be good for either of our images. We kissed in the conference room before making our way to my suite." Solomon stopped. "Wait, what's this all about? Don't tell me you want her?"

Tanner grinned. "Not on your life. But you've solved a mystery for me."

"What kind of mystery?"

"The kind where my girlfriend and the mother of our unborn child gets all bent out of shape over a case of mistaken identity."

Solomon cocked a brow. "She thought I was you?"

Tanner nodded. "Now that you've shaved your head, guess we look more alike than I realized."

"You want me to talk to her?"

"I've got a better idea," Tanner said thoughtfully, hoping that it would finally set the record straight and give him and Bianca a chance to put this behind them so they could move forward with the life together they both richly deserved.

Bianca wondered what it was with men that they could so easily lie even in the face of overwhelming evidence. In this case, what she saw with her own eyes spoke for itself. So why did Tanner act like she was crazy and attempt to profess his innocence?

*What else would he say when I caught him with his hand in the cookie jar?* she asked herself.

She couldn't continue to be in a relationship with someone who clearly still had the playboy in him and could just fall back on it whenever things were strained between them.

Leave it to someone like Kendre Kelly to capitalize on an opportunity to get a man she wanted. The fact that he fell for it spoke for itself, in spite of Tanner's weak denials to the contrary.

Bianca went into the kitchen. She wanted to have a glass of wine, but knew that it wouldn't be good for the baby. Instead, she poured some cranberry juice into a glass, taking a sip as she tried to figure out how to get over the man she still loved.

The ringing of the doorbell startled her.

She walked to the foyer and looked out the peephole.

Kendre Kelly stood there, wearing sunglasses, as if to hide her identity.

Once she got over the shock of finding the singer and Tanner's new romantic interest at her front door, Bianca opened it.

"What are you doing here?" Bianca asked coldly.

Kendre lifted her glasses to the top of her head. "I came to see you."

Bianca was sure that Tanner had sent her to try and sweet-talk her into forgetting what happened between them—and maybe still was happening. "You wasted your time," Bianca told her.

"Well, it's mine to waste, isn't it?" Kendre snapped back.

"I don't need you to explain why you were making out with my man—"

"That's just it—I wasn't making out with Tanner," Kendre said. "I was kissing Solomon."

Bianca brows lowered skeptically. "Since when did Solomon go bald?"

"You'll have to ask him that. Personally, I think it's sexier. Which is why we got a little crazy and kissed, before getting even crazier. I saw you watching us in the conference room, but thought nothing of it. When Tanner told me you thought I was making out with him, I came to set the record straight."

"Why should I believe you?" Bianca asked, not convinced that the singer was being honest.

"Because I'm telling you the truth. If that isn't enough, maybe you'll believe your own eyes." Kendre removed a cell phone from her purse and showed Bianca several photographs of her and Solomon. "I know Tanner and Solomon look alike as brothers, but they're hardly identical twins."

Bianca agreed. The pictures were clearly of a bald-headed Solomon and not Tanner. But, at a glance, she might have mistaken one for the other.

Which is exactly what she had done when she spotted Solomon kissing Kendre.

"Anyway, there's your proof," Kendre said. "Do whatever you want with it. If I were you, though, I'd swallow my pride and go to Tanner. He's really a good man and he's obviously in love with you. If you can't see that, then shame on you." She put her sunglasses back on. "Later."

Bianca watched her sashay away toward a limousine that wasn't Tanner's. All she could think of was that she had made a terrible mistake misjudging him.

Was it too late to make amends? Or would Tanner be the bigger person and let her back into his heart?

## Chapter 26

Tanner was in his office when his secretary informed him that Bianca was waiting outside to see him.

He had hoped she would show up, if not call, and that things could get back on the right path for them. But his business was gambling, and he knew it hadn't been a sure bet, even if he appeared to have a winning hand.

Now it seemed the time had come for both of them to show their cards.

"Send her in," he said.

Tanner remained at his desk as Bianca walked through the door. She was as striking as ever. That much would never change, no matter what went down between them.

"Hey," he said casually.

"Solomon told me I'd find you here," she said.

"Yeah, the business of running a hotel-casino never ends."

She walked up to his desk. "I talked to Kendre. Actually, she did most of the talking, and I listened."

He met her eyes. "So what did you come up with?"

Bianca paused. "It wasn't you I saw kissing her."

"That much we can both agree on," he said smoothly. "She's definitely not my type."

"I feel like such an idiot." Bianca turned her gaze away. "I shouldn't have doubted you."

"I can see how you might have confused a bald Solomon with me, if you saw him from a distance," Tanner said.

"But that's no excuse for jumping to all the wrong conclusions. I should have known that you had more integrity than that." She met his eyes. "Maybe because the men in my past relationships all proved to be jerks, I found it easy to lump you into that category. I'm so sorry."

"It's fine," Tanner said, standing. "You're entitled to make a mistake every now and then, just as I am. We're both human and when we're caught up in emotions, sometimes we misread situations that arise."

Bianca smiled thinly. "So you forgive me?"

He grinned. "Yes, I forgive you."

"Thank you!" She sucked in a breath. "So where do we go from here?"

Tanner stared at the question for a moment, not wanting to mess this up while he had her full attention. "Well, that all depends."

"On…" she asked tentatively.

"On whether or not we both play our cards right."

Bianca raised a brow. "I'm not a gambler, remember?"

"Neither am I," he told her. "At least, not in the official sense. As I told you, I only like to bet on sure things."

"Do you think that applies to us?"

"I'd like to think so, at the end of the day." On that note, Tanner opened the credenza behind him and took out a box of roses. "Will you accept these from me?"

She smiled, reaching out for them. "Yes." She put the flowers to her nose and smelled them. "Thank you."

He smiled, a warm feeling coursing through him. His gaze turned serious as he said, "I should have come out with this the moment it hit me, but I tried to let my actions speak for me." He paused. "I love you, Bianca Wagner. You mean the world to me, and I'd like nothing better than for us to make a great life together—for us and our child."

"I feel the same way," she said. "I've been in love with you for a while, and I just wish I had woken you up to tell you."

"Well, I'm awake now and I hear you," he said affectionately. "It's like music to my ears."

She chuckled. "Then I'll say it again. I love you, Tanner, even though I may have had a funny way of showing it lately."

Tanner smiled while hiding the nervousness he felt over what would come next. He reached into his pocket and pulled out an engagement ring, then fell to one knee and took Bianca's hand.

"Love can only be serious," he told her sincerely. He slid the ring on her finger.

Bianca studied the white-gold ring with a one-carat princess-cut diamond center stone bordered by round accent diamonds.

"It's incredible," she said with awe.

"The two blue sapphires in the ring's bezel symbolize faithfulness and a lifetime of love," noted Tanner, raising his eyes to hers. "Will you marry me, Bianca, so we can take our love to a whole new level for us and our child?"

She held his gaze with watery eyes. "Yes, Tanner, I'll marry you." She rubbed her stomach. "Or, *we* will."

He laughed. "Good thing you can speak for both of you. In the process, you've made me the happiest man in Vegas, if not the entire world!"

"And you've definitely made me the happiest woman on the entire planet!" she exclaimed.

Tanner rose to his feet. "Shall we seal the deal?"

"You'd better." Bianca gave him a big smile and raised her chin, waiting for the kiss.

He delivered, holding her face and giving her a passionate kiss, though saving an even better one for their wedding.

Bianca was seven months pregnant when she and Tanner spent their honeymoon at a hotel in the Kaanapali Beach Resort on the Hawaiian island of Maui.

They'd had a spectacular wedding at the Aloha Seas. Her sister, Madison, was matron of honor and Tanner chose Solomon as his best man. Madison's daughters, Carrie and Dottie, were the flower girls. Both Bianca's parents had flown in. In her mind, it was the perfect wedding, complete with a designer gown and a very handsome groom who made her feel like the most beautiful and loved woman in the world.

When the pastor told Tanner he could kiss the bride, he laid one on Bianca the likes of which she had never felt before. It caused her toes to tingle and went right up her body, leaving her breathless, lightheaded and more in love than ever.

Now they were on a Hawaiian island, cementing the start of their lives as husband and wife by taking in the beauty and atmosphere of Maui and passing it along to their unborn child.

Bianca held Tanner's hand as they took a beach walk, admiring the golden sand and splendor of the Pacific Ocean.

"Now, this is living," Tanner remarked.

"So now you want to live here?" Bianca half joked.

"Maybe not on a permanent basis—but yes, I could certainly see us having a vacation home in Maui."

"You'll get no argument from me there."

He grinned. "Didn't think so."

Bianca watched an attractive, slender young Hawaiian woman pass by, offering a smile at her.

"Are you sure you don't want to trade your very pregnant wife for one of these gorgeous, sexy ladies with perfect bodies?" she teased Tanner.

"Not a chance," he told her. "Believe me, no one is more beautiful on this island than a pregnant woman, especially the one carrying my child."

Bianca grinned. "Good answer."

"I always aim to please," Tanner said with a chuckle. "Especially you."

"Well, you manage to succeed every time."

"That's because I want only the best for you and will make it my business to see that you get it."

"I do have the best in you," she told him sincerely, knowing anything else paled by comparison.

His face lit up. "The same is true in reverse, and I'll never let you forget that."

Bianca suddenly felt like being alone with her sexy man. "Do you want to go back to our suite?"

He cast a loving glance at her. "Do you have to ask?"

She beamed, well aware that their minds seemed to always be in sync when it came to intimacy. Oblivious to everyone else, they made their way back to the hotel, to their home away from home.

There, as man and wife, they made the most of the setting and each other, knowing that this was one bet on love neither could ever lose.

\* \* \* \* \*

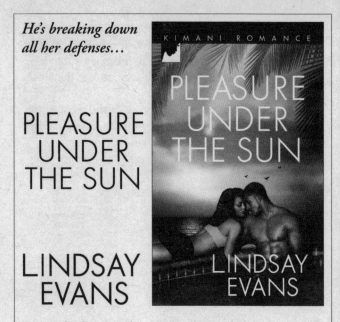

# REQUEST YOUR FREE BOOKS!

## 2 FREE NOVELS PLUS 2 FREE GIFTS!

KIMANI™ ROMANCE

### Love's ultimate destination!